RIDDLE ME THIS

Linda Newbery

CAMBRIDGESHIRE LIBRARIES

JUN 1995

MB

YOUNG ADULTS

Lions
An Imprint of HarperCollins*Publishers*

First published in Great Britain in Lions in 1993
1 3 5 7 9 10 8 6 4 2

Lions is an imprint of the Children's Division,
part of HarperCollins Publishers Ltd
77-85 Fulham Palace Road
Hammersmith, London W6 8JB

Copyright © 1993 Linda Newbery

PB ISBN 0 00 674763 9
HB ISBN 0 00185511 5
The author asserts the moral right to be identified
as author of this work.

Printed and bound in Great Britain by
HarperCollins Manufacturing, Glasgow

Conditions of Sale
This book is sold subject to the condition
that is shall not, by way of trade or otherwise,
be lent, re-sold, hired out or otherwise circulated
without the publisher's prior consent in any form of
binding or cover other than that in which it is
published and without a similar condition
including this condition being imposed
on the subsequent purchaser

Contents

O wise men, riddle me this: what if the
      dream come true?
What if the dream come true? and if
      millions unborn shall dwell
In the house that I shaped in my heart,
      the noble house of my thoughts?

Patrick Pearse

Catherine preferred the open deck to the stuffy warmth of the passenger lounge. The wind whipped strands of her hair loose from their pins and lashed them against her face and neck, and her straw hat tugged at the firmly-tied scarf which restrained it, as if it would take off and soar with the gulls which had followed the boat all the way from Holyhead. She raised a hand to steady the flapping brim and squinted into the late-afternoon sunlight which glanced off the water. The hazy, undulating silhouette of the Wicklow Mountains was already in view, and the Howth Peninsula stretched out like an arm cradling Dublin Bay. Soon she would see Kingstown Harbour, and then, if she had been able to see through a belt of woodland and over a rise, and if she had had a powerful long-range telescope, she would have been able to see Mullaghcleevaun House. She always pretended she could see it anyway, fixing her gaze in the direction she supposed it to be; it was one of her coming-home rituals. The grey-tiled house would be hung with wisteria, faded from its early summer splendour, and the cedar of Lebanon would cast deep shade over the lawn. Home was always reassuringly the same, an unchanging, self-contained world, even through the years of the war. Catherine knew from experience that later in the summer it would seem too much the same; she would miss her school friends and find her home too dull. But now she thought fondly of tea beneath the cedar, and Father's roses on the hall table, and Mother in her elegant pale dresses, and Aunt Madge's countless cats, and the long leisurely days without prep or bells or sharp-voiced prefects.

In the Wicklow Hills, a young man was walking slowly towards a rounded summit. His eyes were fixed on the meandering path in front of him and he placed his feet carefully, not looking up. Pale moths skittered, disturbed by the brushing of his boots against the dry heather. The skylarks irritated him, burbling on in their stupid mindless way, filling his head with their noise and interfering with his concentration. He must keep walking until he reached the summit and then he would have to force himself to stand there, exposed, resisting the impulse which had been shrieking at him, ever since he left the shelter of the trees, to get down, take cover.

One foot after the other. Try not to think any further ahead than the next step. That was the way to do it.

Someone was waiting in the thick cover of shrubs behind the gardener's cottage.

He had hardly moved for the last hour and a half. The uneventful wait did not bother him; he was expert at switching off one part of his mind, while another part noted every movement in the windows and doorways of the house: a servant girl shaking a cloth out of the kitchen door, figures moving into the dining room, a window opening upstairs.

At last he saw what he had been waiting for. A figure in evening dress, a young man, emerged from the porch at the front of the house and strolled down the long-shadowed lawns, then paused obligingly beneath the cedar of Lebanon to light up a cigarette, providing a clear view. He was close enough for the observer to hear the striking of a match and to see the flame against the flesh-glow of a cupped hand.

The watcher in the shadows stood perfectly still, making less movement than the laurel leaves which swayed gently in the merest breath of wind. Mentally, he checked off the details against those he had memorised. He waited until the young man had ambled on down the lawn towards the pond and ornamental bridge, and then he ghost-footed round to the back of the gardener's cottage and slipped away into the dusk.

Mullaghcleevaun

Mullaghcleevaun House greeted Catherine in its best clothes, its full summer luxuriance. The elders and seed-grass of the lane gave way to the mown lawns and carefully tended shrubberies and borders of the garden. In the fragrant dusk the house seemed like a living presence, the lamps in the downstairs windows shining out a welcome. The car tyres crunched into the gravel, and Catherine saw the tall figure of her mother rising to her feet in the drawing room.

Paddy Kerrigan brought the Vauxhall to a halt outside the front door and left the engine idling.

"Here you are then, miss. Home itself."

"Thank you, Paddy." Catherine jumped down from the passenger door. Her mother had come out to the porch, where she stood gracefully silhouetted against the light from inside and framed by the climbing roses which scrambled over the stone arch.

"Catherine, darling!" She clasped Catherine in a perfumed hug, kissed her on both cheeks and then held her at arm's length to look at her. "You look well, my darling. You've grown a little plumper, I think? A little rounder in the face? Come inside, darling. Paddy will bring your bags in."

"Nonsense, Delia. Don't tease the girl. She looks healthy, not plump." Catherine's father had followed his wife to the front door, walking heavily. His face was tanned and weathered by hours in the garden. "Catherine – ah – " He came up to her to present his cheek for a kiss and she breathed in his familiar smell of coal-tar soap and cigar smoke. For a second, in the awkwardness of first meeting, it seemed that he could think of nothing to say to her. Then he asked gruffly, "A good crossing?"

"Yes, perfectly calm, thank you. Maura hardly spoke to me – I can't think why you make us travel together, it's exactly like being on my own – Andrew!"

Catherine's half-brother, who had paused in the drawing-room doorway, came forward to greet her. He hugged her briefly, carefully holding his lit cigar away from her. "Hello, little sister."

He looked unfamiliar in a dinner jacket, older than his twenty-five years, stockier in build and more like their father than she remembered. She had seen little of him during the war or since, their visits home rarely coinciding, and she felt suddenly shy of his maturity and self-possession.

"You look older," she said.

He laughed. "Well, I am older. And so are you, little sister. You're looking quite the young lady."

"I should say she is," their father said proudly. "She'll be just as beautiful as her mother one of these days. Won't she, Delia, my dear?"

It was another of the rituals of Catherine's homecomings: discussing how much she had grown, how much she resembled her mother. Catherine couldn't see herself ever turning into a figure as striking as her mother, who now raised a hand to smooth a loose strand of hair into place with her characteristic grace of movement, and said vaguely, "Oh, yes, I'm sure she will. Now, Catherine, Patsy has saved you some supper. Come into the dining room and she can unpack your bags upstairs while you eat it."

"I can eat in the kitchen with Patsy," Catherine said.

"Nonsense, darling. Come into the dining room and I'll talk to you meanwhile. We'll join your father and Andrew as soon as you've eaten."

Catherine obediently washed her hands and face in the downstairs cloakroom and joined her mother in the dining room. The house had electricity now, but the soft globes around the dining-room walls looked just as they had in the days of gas lighting. A mahogany dresser on which Delft china was displayed rose impressively almost to the ceiling. On the wall opposite Catherine was a portrait of her father in military uniform, a memento of his army years in India before he had married for the second time and inherited the Irish estate. The scent of roses hung in the air from a bowl of pale pink blooms on the sideboard. One petal had fallen and lay on the polished surface like a discarded shell; Catherine's mother picked it up in a gesture of automatic tidying, and then sat at the table rolling and unrolling it in her long fingers while the housekeeper came in with the late meal.

"Sure, she's turning into a regular young lady!" Patsy McCabe exclaimed. "And don't you think she's looking more and more like yourself, Mrs Enright?"

Catherine's mother waited almost impatiently while Patsy served the food, not replying. Catherine, knowing that she would have a good long chat with Patsy next day in the kitchen, began immediately on her supper.

"I didn't expect Andrew to be here," she remarked.

"Oh, yes," her mother said. "He's on leave until next week."

"I thought he would have wanted to come out of the army as soon as the war was over. Will he go out to India, like Father?"

"No, darling. He's taking up a new post in Dublin, starting next week. And another surprise for you – Martin's staying, too."

Catherine darted a look at her mother. "Martin, staying here? When's he coming?"

"Oh, he's here already. He went out for a stroll after dinner. I'm sure he'll be in soon – he knows you're expected, of course."

Catherine did not reply for fear that her voice would give her away. If only she'd known – she'd wasted all that time on the journey when she could have been counting the hours . . .

"But, Catherine – " Her mother looked down at the bruised rose petal between her fingers. "You may find him a bit – well, not quite himself. He's been ill recently. Your aunt and uncle thought it would do him good to have a few weeks of relaxation, away from everything. Of course we're delighted to have him. But I'm glad to have had this chance to warn you – be careful what you say to him."

Catherine stopped eating. "What's the matter with him?"

"It's difficult to say. Not the sort of illness that can be diagnosed."

"You mean it's something serious?"

9

"No, no. Hardly a physical illness at all. It's some sort of delayed shock – from the war, you know the sort of thing. Something he can't seem to put behind him. He was perfectly all right until he came home, apparently. Now he can't settle to anything, can't seem to make decisions about his future – you know he was supposed to be going into publishing with his father. When did you last see him?"

Catherine knew, to the day – Christmas Eve, 1917 – but she made a show of casting about in her memory. "It must have been in London, that Christmas at Aunt Margaret's. Two years ago, or was it three? He'd managed to get leave at the last minute."

A picture slipped into her mind of Martin getting out of a taxi in his officer's uniform, straightening up from paying the driver, looking at her blankly for a few seconds and then smiling in recognition. It was the first time she'd seen him in uniform; it suited him so well that she was struck by the glamour of his appearance. But then he'd come indoors bringing with him a smell which was far from glamorous: sweat, and mud, and something else indefinably unpleasant. Aunt Margaret had sent him straight upstairs to change into his own clothes and she had bundled up the uniform, holding it at arm's length as if it would contaminate her, and had given it to the manservant to clean. Had Martin looked ill then? Catherine could only remember the occasional vacant expression when people spoke to him. Perhaps that was what her mother meant. She remembered that he had looked thin, even gaunt, but at the time she had attributed that to poor cooking in the army. She had been too young to understand more than that. The war had been going on in the background for so long that she had been surprised when it ended; she had come to accept it as an inevitable part of life, and one which hadn't affected her personally very much, in the cloistered environment of her Surrey boarding school. Yet if she had been a few years older, and male . . .

"Poor Martin," she said.

"Yes. I keep thinking that we're . . . well! It could have been Andrew. We've been lucky."

She looked up at Catherine, who saw the perfect oval of her face, the vivid blue eyes, and the swept-up hair without a trace of grey. How could people think they were alike?

"It will be good for him to have your company," her mother continued. "We must do all we can to give him a pleasant stay."

Catherine nodded, picking up her knife and fork. "Of course. But why did you think I might be tactless?"

Her mother's manner became brisk again.

"Well, you know. With Andrew having been at the front too, it's not a good subject to bring up. It's unfortunate, in a way, that Andrew got leave at the same time." She stood up and smoothed the skirt of her dress. "Finish your meal, darling, and I'll go and ask Patsy to bring us more coffee when you've had your pudding. I'm sure Martin will have come in by then."

Catherine continued to eat, thinking about the unexpected turn her arrival home had taken. Andrew, and Martin too . . . It would certainly make the summer considerably more interesting than it would have been otherwise. Poor Martin . . . Vague pictures of mud and trenches came into her mind. All she knew about conditions in the army and at the western front came from *The Illustrated London News*, or from the conversations of girls at school whose brothers were in the armed forces. Andrew had been in the army since early 1915, but had said little to her about his experiences, and the letters he had sent her had been brief and factual. Perhaps Martin would tell her what it had really been like.

She ate slowly, wanting to see Martin, but apprehensive. Would he look strange? Behave oddly? She thought again of their last meeting, which had made her aware of Martin in a new and exciting way, as someone facing unimaginable danger. But the war hadn't finished for another eleven months after that, and he had been due to go straight back to his unit in Belgium. Anything could have happened to him in that time . . .

Across the table, her eyes met the challenging gaze of her father in the portrait. It reminded her suddenly of Andrew; her father could not have been much older than Andrew when the portrait had been done. There were distinct similarities in the light hazel-coloured eyes, the firm line of the jaw, the stocky build. Andrew, son of their father's first marriage, took strongly after him; Catherine was more like her mother, having the same dark hair and blue eyes, although there, she thought, the resemblance ended. Andrew had followed his father into the army and would eventually succeed him as owner of the Mullagh-cleevaun estate. As for her own future, people seemed to expect her to turn out as graceful and poised as her mother, as if that were an end in itself. It was different for a girl, but Catherine did not feel any confidence that she could succeed, even in that limited aim.

Patsy McCabe

Catherine was tired from her journey, and slept late. By the time she was dressed and downstairs, everyone else had finished breakfast long ago, so she had hers in the kitchen with Patsy McCabe, which, secretly, she preferred. There were plenty of scrambled eggs and the bread came in thicker slices than in the dining room, and she could help herself to as much butter as she liked instead of being constrained to moderation by the delicate ribbed curls arranged on a chilled plate. One day, if her mother had her way, as she usually did, Catherine would go to finishing school in Switzerland to learn etiquette, and would be affronted if anyone served her tea in a workman-like plain white cup and saucer rather than fluted bone china. But now she was enjoying her breakfast.

"It's good to have you back again, so it is," Patsy remarked, refilling the teapot at the range. "It'll be grand to have young voices around the house again, with you and Mr Andrew – Major

Enright, I should call him now – and your cousin all here."

From Catherine's point of view, Andrew was so far advanced into adulthood that his could hardly be classed as a young voice, and judging by the short time she had spent with Martin last night she could hardly imagine that he would be contributing much in the way of youthful gaiety. It had been an awkward meeting, and disappointing; Martin had said little, excusing himself early, and Catherine had been so conscious of her mother's presence that she had been frozen into shyness.

"Martin seemed very quiet last night," she remarked. "But then, Mother does tend to run everyone's conversations for them."

Patsy smiled as she replaced the teapot on the table, but made no comment. Whatever her private opinions might be, Catherine knew that she would never be disloyal to her employers by agreeing with even the slightest criticism.

"Do you know what happened to him?" Catherine persevered. "In the war, I mean?"

Patsy returned to the big mixing bowl where she was kneading pastry. "It mightn't have been one particular thing. Maybe it was just the war itself. It's a terrible thing to have to go through so young. What surprises me is that there weren't more affected that way. Though you can never tell what goes on in a person's head. Still it's a pity now that young Mr Sheringham broke off his engagement and all. A happy marriage might have been just the thing to help him over it."

"He's broken off his engagement?" Catherine looked up at Patsy, who was frowning in concentration over the kneading. "Did Mother tell you that? She didn't say anything about it last night."

"Perhaps the poor fellow doesn't want it talked about. A lovely young lady she was by all accounts."

Patsy broke off small pieces of pastry and began to roll them out for tartlets. Catherine buttered another piece of bread, intrigued by the new information. She had never met Martin's fiancée – a girl called Serena Hastings, she knew from her mother's letters – and the fact that the romance was now over seemed satisfactory rather than distressing. Martin's restoration to normality had become, overnight, Catherine's project for the summer holiday. If he had had a fiancée in England he would probably not have been here, or at the very least he would be writing to her, sharing confidences which Catherine wanted to be hers alone. She had always felt rather resentful towards the unknown Serena.

Admittedly, last night had not been a promising start. She reminded herself that Martin had last seen her as a girl of twelve or thirteen, in pigtails. Now he had to get used to the idea that she was nearly grown-up. She hoped it would be easier when she could talk to him alone, away from her mother's watchful eye.

"Where are Martin and Andrew now?" she asked casually.

A row of greased trays for the tartlets stood ready on the table. Patsy flipped the pastry bases in and pressed them down with deft floured fingers. "Mr – Major Enright has taken the car into Dublin, and I think Mr Sheringham has gone out into the woods with your father."

Too late to catch Martin this morning, then. Catherine thought of her other childhood play-mate, Conor Kerrigan, son of Paddy who had always done the gardening and now turned his hand to chauffeuring and car maintenance when required.

"I wonder if Conor's anywhere around?" she remarked. "Father told me he'd come back from Doneraile."

Patsy looked at her. "Yes, he's an apprentice blacksmith, with Jimmy Doyle. But I wouldn't be after seeing so much of Conor as you used to when you were small. Things are different now."

"Why? Why does everything have to be different? I want everything the same."

Her voice rang plaintively in her ears, like a child's.

"You can't go back, Catherine my dear," Patsy said tolerantly. "Nor even stay in the one place. Times change. You're getting to be a young lady now and Conor has his own way to make in the world."

"Is that all you meant?"

"Well – he's a new way of looking at things, since living with his cousins out in the west."

Catherine sensed that there was some significance to Conor having been in Doneraile, something which eluded her, and which Patsy wasn't revealing. She was disappointed. Patsy was usually the one person she could turn to for explanations when other adults told her she was too young to understand, or used other vague fobbings-off. Now it seemed that Patsy was doing the same.

"What, then? What's made him change?"

Patsy said, "It's been hard in that family. With the mother gone, and Fergal killed in the war. It's hit Conor hard, losing his brother. He's a different boy now."

"The war again," Catherine murmured. The war seemed to cast long shadows, longer, perhaps, than she had realised before.

Patsy disappeared for a moment into the larder and then emerged with two bottles of redcurrants. "There's no getting away from it. Just be glad it's over now. I was mightily glad my own boy hadn't good enough eyesight to enlist, him being of military age."

Catherine watched as she filled the tartlets with glossy fruit and then rolled thin pastry strips for a lattice decoration. Patsy had been housekeeper to the Enrights for as long as Catherine could remember, but for the first time Catherine realised how little she knew of her personal background beyond a few basic facts. She knew that Patsy had been widowed ten years ago in her mid-thirties and had a grown-up son in Dublin, but through all the years of the war it had never occurred to her to wonder how Patsy would have felt if her son joined the army. Patsy had simply been there, quietly and efficiently going about her work, providing a sympathetic ear when required. She was one of the unchanging working parts of Mullaghcleevaun which made the house run smoothly. And yet, it seemed, there had been changes, of which Catherine had been unaware.

"Yes," Patsy concluded, "it's bitter for Paddy Kerrigan to lose a son over there in the English war."

Catherine made the necessary mental adjustment. The English pupils at Kingswood House thought she was as Irish as shamrock or the

Blarney Stone, but here in Ireland it was different. She and her family were Anglo-Irish, not the same thing at all.

At Kingswood House School, the war had been talked about obsessively at first. Any girl who had a brother or other close relative in the army was treated with special respect, as if the strange glamour clung to her of being associated with someone who might soon be dead. And fairly soon, after the retreat from Mons, a girl in one of the upper forms was called to the headmistress's office and summoned home by telegram. News had arrived that her brother had been killed.

This, the first death directly affecting a member of the school community, was given special significance. Prayers were read in assembly for the girl and her family. When she returned to school after special leave of absence and was seen going about the corridors with eyes downcast and saddened, the younger girls treated her with a reverence which bordered on adulation, as if she had been martyred. But by the time Andrew went to the front for the first time in the autumn of 1915, Catherine found that no special attentions came her way. It was commonplace by now to have a brother in the armed forces. Some girls had two or even three.

By this time the war no longer aroused any special excitement, and simply became the accepted background to the routines of bells and prep and mealtimes and bedtimes. Knitting socks and Balaclava helmets for the troops, an enthusiastic contribution to the war effort at first, became a tiresome chore.

By the last year of the war, when the girls in Catherine's form were old enough to take an interest in such things, photographs of grave-faced young officers were displayed on bedside tables in the dormitory. The only photographs permitted were of immediate family, but this rule was treated with a certain amount of flexibility. Catherine thought she was being daring by having Martin's picture by her bed, but one girl had pictures of three junior officers, each of whom she claimed to be in love with her. There was a barter trade in photographs, and even the buzzard-eyed house mistress did not suspect that the framed image kissed every night by Mary Grenville, two places along, was of Captain Andrew Enright.

Catherine kept the photograph of Martin jealously to herself.

Aunt Madge

Great Aunt Madge had separate rooms on the upper floor of the house, where she was looked after by her own maid-companion. Catherine went up to see her after lunch. The curtains were drawn against the fierce afternoon sun so that there was a premature twilight in the room, and the air was warm and thick and smelled unmistakably of cats. A whole wall was taken up with rows of framed photographs, countless faces staring out from the age of Queen Victoria. Aunt Madge sat in a vast cushioned rocking chair, while the English maid, Phyllis, attempted to wedge shoes on to the old lady's unyielding feet.

"Good afternoon, Delia," Aunt Madge said.

"No, it's Catherine," Phyllis corrected. "Home from school."

"Delia," Aunt Madge said again, defiantly, as Catherine bent to kiss her thin cheek.

"We're about to take our afternoon walk," Phyllis explained.

As her eyes adjusted to the gloom, Catherine

began to see the cats. There was one on Aunt Madge's lap, a thin tabby. One was a shadow on the windowsill, against the curtain. A smoke-grey was curled up among the framed photographs on the sideboard, and two gingers were entwined in deep sleep on an armchair. Another sat like a bookend on the shelves regarding Catherine with amber eyes which seemed to communicate some ancient intelligence.

"Come into the garden with us, Delia," Aunt Madge said, rising stiffly to her feet.

"It's no good," Phyllis whispered. "It'll take her three or four days to realise who you are."

"What's that?" Aunt Madge said crossly. "I don't like people whispering. Speak up." She was wearing a thin summer dress which hung loosely from her bony shoulders. It was a style which would have looked elegant on Catherine's mother, but on Aunt Madge it drew attention to the sagging skin of her neck and her jutting collarbone.

"I was just going to say to Catherine how well you've been," Phyllis said, speaking clearly.

"Catherine? Who's Catherine? Come on, cats. Petruchio . . . Minerva . . . puss, puss . . . Juno, my lovely, come . . ." She called each name in a high crooning voice, until the last sleeper was awake and stirring. Cats appeared from concealment around the room to trill at Aunt Madge in pleasurable anticipation and to entwine themselves around Catherine's legs, their fur cool through the thin fabric of her dress. Phyllis opened the door and the three women went slowly down the stairs preceded by a feline surge. On the first landing halfway down, with her face weirdly illuminated by the sunlight shining through red and green stained glass, Aunt Madge stopped and looked at Catherine with candid blue eyes and said, "I saw Edwin in the garden today. I always knew he'd come back."

Catherine, wondering who on earth Aunt Madge thought she was talking about, caught Phyllis's eye over the old lady's shoulder.

"Hush, hush. Come along, now. Not much farther." Phyllis took hold of the elbow which projected from the flimsy dress like the wing of a plucked chicken.

"You don't have to treat me like a baby," Aunt Madge said. "I can manage on my own."

Later that evening Catherine stood in front of the cheval mirror in her room and looked critically at her reflection. The dress she was wearing was a little tight across the chest and short in the sleeve; she wondered whether to ask for some new things. Her mother would be the first to complain if she didn't look her best for social occasions.

The eyes looking back at her from the glass were the same blue as her mother's, and, more disconcertingly, the same as Aunt Madge's. Catherine had a sudden vision of herself old and eccentric, talking nonsense, wearing the wrong kind of clothes that made her look like a scarecrow. Who would look after her? It must be terrible to be old. Perhaps being old was rather like being a child: kept on the edge of things, only partially understanding what was going on around you.

She turned her thoughts to the evening ahead. The Enrights had invited guests for dinner: Maurice and Ingrid Fitzwilliam, and their daughter Maura. The invitation had been made partly on the basis of Delia's false notion that Catherine and Maura were good friends. They were at the same school in England and arrangements were always made for them to travel to and from Surrey together. At school, they came into contact very rarely, since Maura was in the form above Catherine's and was one of a group of sixth-form girls who took themselves very seriously. Catherine considered Maura dull and knew that Maura in turn probably thought her unintelligent and childish. They had exhausted all topics of mutual interest within five minutes of starting out on the train journey to Holyhead.

It was typical of Mother, Catherine thought, to encourage her to spend time with Martin, then arrange the day so that she had hardly seen him, and to top it all invite guests for dinner so that they would have to make polite conversation. A whole day had passed since her arrival and she'd still exchanged hardly more than the odd word with her cousin.

Catherine pushed back a wisp of hair which kept obstinately falling forward, and gave her reflection a final scowl. It was no use thinking that her dark hair and blue eyes made her anything like her mother; those, and her clear complexion, were her only assets. The figure in the glass was rather plump, her mother was right about that; admittedly not ugly but certainly nowhere near beautiful, the dumpy figure of a schoolgirl dressed up in an outdated evening frock that was too small for her. And she knew that as soon as she saw her mother in her finery she would feel even more dowdy and inadequate.

Patsy had been busy all day with the preparations, helped by a new maid Catherine hadn't seen before, a girl of about her own age, who was to wait at table. Catherine had heard Patsy giving instructions: "Don't speak unless you're spoken to . . . Serve the ladies first . . ." and had seen the girl, Bridie, looking more and more nervous. She was pretty, small and slim (attributes Catherine envied), with plentiful reddish hair piled up beneath her cap. Catherine thought she looked rather nice, much more pleasant than Maura Fitzwilliam. And then she remembered what Patsy had said about Conor. He had his own way to make in the world, and so, presumably, did this Bridie. Part of growing up, as Catherine's mother would be sure to see it, was learning to keep a distance from servants. That, she thought, was part of what Patsy had meant about Conor; but only part.

She went down to the drawing room and found that Martin was the only person there, holding a glass of sherry and staring at the bookcase. He turned as she entered and there was an awkward silence. Catherine felt that he was dredging his thoughts for something to say, and was too tongue-tied herself to spare him the effort. His physical presence had such an effect on her that she could only gaze at him.

He managed to speak at last. "Hello, Catherine. You look . . . er . . . charming."

She laughed nervously. "I look a fright. This dress is too small."

"You were a little girl with long plaits when I

27

saw you last, that Christmas. Now ..." He extended a hand as if the gesture summed up the change in her.

"You look different too," Catherine said. "You were practically asleep, you were so tired, and wearing that smelly uniform when you arrived. Do you remember your mother – " She faltered into silence, realising that she had blundered straight into the area of conversation she had been told to avoid. Was she supposed to ignore his army experience, pretend it hadn't happened?

But Martin laughed as if the remark had put him at ease rather than upsetting him, and said, "Yes, I do. She'd have put it straight in the incinerator if she'd had her way. What she didn't realise was that it was actually far cleaner than usual. I'd stopped off at a delousing station on the way back."

"Did you really have lice? I mean – I know the private soldiers did – but you were an officer."

Martin smiled. "Lice were no respecters of rank, I'm afraid. Let me get you a drink."

"I don't usually have it."

"Oh, but now, surely? A small one?"

She accepted, and he went to the decanter and poured sherry into a crystal glass. She took it from him and their fingers touched briefly. She

28

wondered what he would say if he knew about the photograph she had kept in the school dormitory, or that it was upstairs in her room now. It had never occurred to her that the uniform he was wearing in it was full of lice.

He watched her sipping the sherry. "Do you like it?"

"Yes, I do. It's nice – warming."

He reached a hand into the pocket of his dinner jacket for a cigarette tin, and then put it back again. "I suppose I ought not to smoke, not until after dinner."

"I don't mind."

"Thanks, but I'll wait, anyway. I was thinking, if this fine weather lasts it would be nice to go down to the sea. It's not far, is it, by car?"

"No – we could easily get there in less than an hour."

He did not reply, and she immediately wondered whether her impulsive "we" had been misplaced – perhaps he meant that he wanted to go to the sea by himself. She sipped her drink again, looking at his profile. He was leaning against the windowsill to look up at the sky, presumably assessing the weather prospects. His figure in the dark evening suit was slender, with none of Andrew's mature spreading; he was shorter than Andrew, although still a good few inches taller than Catherine. Against the starched white shirt his colouring was striking: dark brown hair, and very dark eyes with clear whites. His features were neat and regular, with a cast to them that could sometimes appear sulky; Catherine found this attractive rather than off-putting. At the moment he looked quite cheerful, normal, not like someone suffering from depression, or shell-shock, or whatever the proper name was for his condition. She felt disappointed; the role she had planned for herself as confidante might be less important than she had imagined. He turned from the window to look at her, and she wondered whether he realised that she had been admiring him.

He said, "I hope I won't get in your way, Catherine. Please don't think you've got to bother with me. I'm not very good company at the moment. I don't want to mess up your summer holiday."

"Of course you won't," she protested. "I'm glad you're staying."

He seemed about to say more, but at that point they heard the crunch of car tyres outside in the drive, and her parents' voices in the hallway. Martin seemed to draw himself together, straightening his shoulders, and from the resigned look on his face she guessed that he felt much the same as she did about the evening ahead.

Roadblock

It was dusk. By a lane leading from the village of Fanagmore and up into the hills behind Mullaghcleevaun, two men stood in the undergrowth which bordered the coniferous woodland on either side, facing each other across the narrow dusty track. They were so well concealed in the shadows that anyone walking or driving along the lane could have passed within a few feet of them without noticing their presence. But no one would get far along the lane in a car that night. A few yards from the watchers, where the track rounded a bend closely fringed by a dense planting of spruce, the roadway was blocked by a tree trunk and branches dragged out from a clearing by a forestry hut.

For a long time there was no movement but a small wisp of woodsmoke curling up above the trees from a cottage chimney down in the village; nothing to hear but the harsh bark of a vixen in the woods. Nevertheless, the two men kept to their positions, not speaking. Then they glanced at each other as the drone of an engine was heard coming from the direction of the village, followed by a momentary slackening and then the higher note of a car climbing the hill in low gear. The man who stood on the outward curve of the bend, placed where he would be first to see the car as it approached, pulled his cap down lower over his forehead and pulled up a scarf tied loosely round his neck so that it muffled his face as far as the bridge of his nose. He nodded to his companion, and tightened his grip, beneath the flap of his jacket, on the handle of a .45 revolver.

At Dinner

Martin had withdrawn from the conversation before the end of the soup course. Now he leaned back in his chair observing the other diners, aware that he was hardly doing his duty as a dinner guest but unwilling to make the effort to do anything about it.

He disliked social occasions, and had been led to believe that his stay in Ireland would free him from any such obligations. He disliked the pretence, the false airs people put on. At the moment, the person who irritated him most was Delia – he couldn't bring himself to think of her as Aunt, and her manner towards him discouraged any such idea. In fact, the longer he remained silent, the more marked her attentions became. And for all his irritation, he couldn't help feeling flattered too.

"... getting harder and harder to find reliable staff these days," Uncle Douglas was complaining. "It's almost more than Kerrigan can manage on his own ..."

Martin thought he'd been imagining it at first, but now thought not: her tinkling laugh, the way she leaned towards him intimately whenever she tried to draw him into conversation so that it was difficult to avert his eyes from her cleavage, the intent looks from her blue eyes, at once suggestive and innocent, all seemed calculated to arouse his interest. It was most un-auntlike behaviour. Of course, she wasn't actually related to him, and everything he'd seen since his arrival suggested that she was bored with her husband.

". . . it's such a comfort to me that the two girls can travel together . . . so nice for them both that they're friends . . ."

Why, he wondered, had Delia married a stick like Uncle Douglas? She was good-looking enough to have taken her pick of admirers in her day. He could only suppose that money and property had played their part. There must be at least fifteen years' difference in age, and the way Delia dressed and behaved created the impression of an even larger gap. He suspected that her main pleasure in dinner parties was to display herself as a beautiful woman and a perfect hostess. It couldn't be coincidence, surely, that she chose to surround herself with plain women? His glance roved around the table. There was that school friend of Catherine's, all teeth and wiry hair. Her mother, Ingrid Fitzwilliam, could only be described as matronly, with large, rather horse-like features . . .

". . . I do hope you'll like this dessert. It's my housekeeper's special recipe . . ."

And then there was Catherine. The poor girl looked distinctly uncomfortable, self-consciously crammed into a dress that looked a couple of sizes too small. With all the attention Delia paid to her own dress and appearance, you'd think she could have provided something better for her daughter. It was almost as if she wanted Catherine to remain a schoolgirl rather than turn into a potential rival. How would Delia have felt if Catherine had turned into a stunning beauty? Not pleased, Martin thought. Still, there was no danger on that score. Catherine was a nice girl and she wouldn't look bad at all once she'd lost some of that puppy fat, but she was never likely to turn men's heads the way her mother did.

". . . Have you seen anything of the Delaunays recently? The eldest son's gone back to India, I believe . . ."

No, Martin decided, the best-looking female in the room apart from Delia was the new maid, Bridie. She was hovering around the edges of the table, biting her lip in her anxiety to do everything right. Not doing too badly, as far as Martin was aware. It was a shame to stuff all that glorious red hair into a maid's cap; he imagined it tumbling around her shoulders when she undressed at night, pale shoulders, lightly freckled like her face . . . While he was thinking this, Catherine caught his eye across the table and smiled at him, a shy, secretive smile. She'd have been shocked if she'd known what he'd been thinking about. But she really was very sweet. He'd forgotten that she was nearly sixteen, not a child any more; it wouldn't be too bad at all, having her around. It was a bonus which almost cancelled out the bad luck of finding that stuffed shirt Andrew at Mullaghcleevaun. He was staying in the army, of course, and would doubtless turn into another Colonel Enright, passing the port and analysing past military campaigns . . .

And then a loud double bang dashed all rational thought out of his head and left only a dizzying black confusion into which he fell and drowned.

Conversation was abruptly halted by the bangs outside, echoing from some way off. Spoons stopped halfway to mouths, fearful glances were exchanged. Catherine's eyes went straight to Martin, who had risen half to his feet, clutching at the tablecloth, his eyes unfocused as if he would pass out. For a second Catherine thought he would fall backwards and pull the whole table-setting with him in a cascade of cut glass and fine china. Everyone else seemed frozen into immobility, staring towards the window. About to dash round the table to steady him, Catherine was forestalled by Bridie, who was there behind him in an instant, taking Martin's shoulders and trying to replace his fallen chair and guide him back into it at the same time. Martin resisted, stiff-limbed, his eyes wild.

"Help her, Mother!" Catherine said sharply, out of her seat.

And then the others seated round the table seemed to notice what was happening for the first time.

"Oh, I say . . ."

"Poor young fellow, of course, I'd forgotten . . ."

"Leave him to me, girl. Fetch the brandy."

"I should take him through to the sofa. Here, let me help . . ."

"No, I can manage."

Andrew had taken control now, half-dragging Martin away from the table, waving Catherine out of the way. She watched, appalled. The colonel flapped ineffectually, moving chairs aside and making vague gestures towards the door.

"It's just the shock, the sudden noise." Delia smoothly reverted to her hostess manner. "But he's seemed so much better since he's been here. Didn't you think so, Douglas? Now sit down, Catherine. It won't do any good to have all of us bustling round."

"Let me help. I could fetch a blanket," Catherine appealed.

"No, no, darling. Andrew can cope, and the girl will fetch whatever's needed. I'm sure Martin will feel better in a moment or two. Perhaps an early night would be best for him."

The drama of Martin's collapse had distracted attention from the source of the noise outside. Now everyone began to discuss it at once.

"It could easily be poachers," the colonel said. "I've an idea that Conor Kerrigan's been snaring rabbits in our woods."

"Don't be absurd, dear," his wife replied briskly. "Snaring rabbits is one thing. Firing guns near the house at night-time is another. If it was poachers, then it certainly wasn't Conor. Our gardener's son," she explained to the guests.

"Perhaps it would be a good idea to telephone the police," Maura said.

"Probably farther away than it sounded. Could easily be a mile or so away. Sounds carry on a quiet summer evening like this," the colonel said, readjusting scattered cutlery.

"An engine backfiring, perhaps?" Mrs Fitzwilliam suggested. "They can make quite a startling noise. A motor-bicycle backfired near me once and I nearly fainted with shock."

"Christopher Delaunay told me the other day," her husband said slowly, "that his manservant was tied up overnight in an outhouse by Sinn Feiners, and threatened with shooting. He handed in his notice the next day. He was terrified out of his wits."

Everyone was momentarily silenced by the mention of Sinn Feiners. It seemed to Catherine that it was the one possibility for the explosions that no one wanted to hear. Surely it can't have been a shooting, she thought; that sort of thing doesn't happen in quiet places like this, away from the big towns . . .

"But how dreadful. Why would they pick on a manservant?" Delia said.

Mr Fitzwilliam shrugged. "A manservant in a Protestant household, where the older son's in the army . . . maybe the Sinn Feiners thought he was informing on them."

"Really," Delia said, "things do seem to be getting quite ridiculously out of hand in some parts of the country. One would have thought the authorities could manage to control a few hooligans with guns. We've just won a war, after all."

"I don't think it's as simple as that," Maura said. "The Irish fought in the war, too – you can't blame them for wanting to govern their own country. And sending in those Black and Tans from England to keep order only seems to be stirring things up even more. It's easy to underestimate the strength of feeling."

Catherine saw her mother's raised eyebrows before Mrs Fitzwilliam said crisply, "Well, dear, however can you be any judge of that? It seems to me that it's just as easy to overestimate it. As Delia says, it really is just a few ruffians."

Maura did not reply. Mrs Fitzwilliam plucked at her husband's sleeve and said, "Maurice – if there are Shinners about, is it going to be safe to drive home?"

Catherine saw her mother's small frown before her social obligations took over. "But of course," she said smoothly, "you must stay the night if there's any doubt in your minds about driving. We can easily have the spare guest rooms made ready."

"But you've already got poor Mr Sheringham to look after," Mrs Fitzwilliam pointed out.

"I can get Kerrigan to drive up the road and see what's going on," the colonel said. "There's probably nothing to worry about at all. We've had very little trouble of that kind. Poachers, that's the most likely explanation, to my mind. Where's that girl? I'll get her to take a note to

Kerrigan while we have our port. Are you ladies going to adjourn?"

"Bridie went out with Martin," Catherine reminded him. "I think I heard feet going upstairs."

"Be a good girl and go and fetch her," Delia said, turning to Catherine. "Tell her to bring coffee into the drawing room. I'm sure Andrew can deal with Martin by himself."

Catherine, finding the drawing room empty, went upstairs to Martin's room. The servant girl Bridie was just coming out, closing the door with painstaking gentleness. She turned as Catherine approached and caught her breath in surprise.

"It's only me," Catherine said, conscious that she had never spoken to the girl before. "How is he?"

"He's quiet now, miss. The poor young gentleman." Bridie's voice was low and musical. "He started to come to himself a bit while we were getting him up the stairs. Captain Andrew's given him some brandy and something to make him sleep, and he says he'll stay with him until he goes off." Her eyes were wide with concern, her expression full of sympathy. Catherine felt jealous of her for having been in Martin's bedroom, tending to him when he needed help, while she herself had been pushed aside. Bridie's eyes scanned Catherine's face for a moment and then she suddenly seemed embarrassed to have spoken at such length. She bobbed a curtsey and turned to pick up a tray with a brandy bottle and glass on it from a low table by the door.

"Thank you, Bridie," Catherine said.

"Sure, it was no trouble at all, miss. There's little enough anyone can do."

Catherine remembered to tell her about the coffee. She wondered whether to knock on Martin's bedroom door, decided against it, and returned downstairs feeling redundant. From the landing window she saw twin beams of light as a motor car passed in front of the house: the Vauxhall, she supposed, with Paddy Kerrigan at the wheel. What was the point of sending him out into the night, she wondered, if there were gunmen around? Suppose he were shot at himself – how would that help the situation?

Later, when the Fitzwilliams were on the verge of deciding that it might, after all, be best to stay the night, Paddy Kerrigan returned with the news that a Royal Irish Constabulary man had been shot dead on the hill behind the house.

A Day in Dublin

Catherine woke soon after dawn, roused by the early light and the loud cawing of rooks in the garden. She lay for a while thinking over the events of the night before. Martin's room was next to hers; would he be lying awake too, or sleeping in drug-induced stupor, or sweating in some horrible nightmare? She listened, but could hear no sound. Eventually she got up and opened her curtains. The light was hazy, promising another fine day. Past the clear outlines of the Lebanon cedar, pale mist hung over the pond and the ornamental bridge. Woodpigeons cooed in the plantation beyond. She felt a flash of sympathy for the unknown RIC man, who had not lived to see this summer morning. He had been visiting relatives in a house farther up the hill, the police had said when they called late last night; he went there regularly at the same time each week, so the gunmen had known exactly where to wait for him. Catherine knew of the sporadic outbreaks of violence over the last year or so – policemen and soldiers shot dead, an attempt to assassinate the Viceroy – but this was the first time an incident had taken place quite so close to home. All the same, it seemed to have little to do with her and her family; the two sides, Republicans and authorities, were fighting it out, as they had done throughout history, but there was no need for ordinary people to get involved.

Meanwhile, it was too lovely a morning to waste by pointlessly trying to sleep. Catherine got up, washed at the basin and dressed quickly, taking an old pair of laced boots from her wardrobe – the grass would be wet – and a woollen shawl. In case Martin were asleep, she let herself out of the door as silently as she could and tiptoed downstairs, stopping in the porch to put on her boots.

Outside, the air was like spring water, fresher than it had been for days. Every leaf and blade of grass sparkled with dew. Catherine's boots left a trail across the damp lawn as she made her way under the cedar and down towards the pond. She stood for a few moments watching the shadowy movements of fish below the lily-strewn surface, and then went on towards the wicket-gate which led into the plantation. A sweet, heady scent reached her as she went through; the lime trees at the outer edge of the garden were so thickly clustered with yellow-green flowers that the branches seemed to droop with their weight. It was worth getting up early, she thought, to be outside at this most peaceful time of day, untarnished by human affairs.

The plantation of beech and silver birch trees interspersed with conifers held the cool air; a shaft of early sunlight speared down like a natural spotlight. Instinctively moving quietly, Catherine made hardly a sound apart from the occasional twig cracking underfoot. She had walked some distance along the track when her eye was caught by a movement in the undergrowth close by.

For the first time it occurred to her how incredibly foolish it was to walk about on her own when a shooting had taken place a matter of hours before, and to go into the depths of the woods of all places, where no one would hear if she shouted for help. Her instinct was to run back to the house, but before she had the chance to take flight the movement resolved itself into the figure of a tall youth who backed out of the bushes in front of her and straightened up, looking every bit as startled as she was.

"Oh – " Her heart was thumping and her legs felt too weak to support her, let alone run. She and the young man stared at each other, and her jolted brain registered a soft cloth cap above a tanned face, from which greenish eyes looked at her warily at first, then with recognition. Two dead rabbits dangled limply from the young man's right hand.

She caught her breath and then laughed with relief. "Conor! You nearly frightened the life out of me!" The face was both familiar and unfamiliar, and he was much taller than she remembered, so that for a moment she thought she was mistaken, and that this was Conor's elder brother. But then she realised that Fergal was dead, and that this must indeed be Conor.

He smiled back at her, revealing white, slightly crooked teeth. "Miss Catherine! Sure, you gave me quite a shock myself. I heard you were home. It's grand to see you." He looked down at the rabbits and gave an embarrassed half-shrug, and smiled again, sheepishly. "There's no use trying to hide them."

"It's all right. I shan't tell my father. I think he knows, anyway."

"I think he does, too. Isn't it an odd thing now – he knows, and I know he knows, and it's all right so long as he doesn't catch me at it. Then he'd raise the seven devils."

He pronounced it divils, and she smiled at hearing the well-remembered phrase. It seemed years since she had seen him. She realised that she had not spoken to him since the news had come about his brother's death on the Somme. She felt suddenly shy; he was clearly a man now rather than a boy, tall and broad-shouldered, with stubble shadowing his jaw and upper lip.

They had begun to walk slowly along the path together, side by side, but now he stopped and looked at her properly. She hoped he wouldn't say how much she had grown and how much she looked like her mother. In fact he didn't say anything at all, so that she felt embarrassed by his steady regard. She remembered his green eyes but had never before noticed how unusual they were: green flecked with brown, almost amber in this light.

"I hear you're working at the blacksmith's now," she said.

"I am. It's a good job. I didn't want to go into service. And you – Patsy tells me you'll be going off to Switzerland in another year or so. They'll be after turning you into a lady."

"I don't think I'll be very good at being a lady."

"Sure, you'll learn right enough."

She was aware of a distance between them that hadn't existed when they were younger. As a child, she had been able to come home from school and pick up her friendly, teasing relationship with Conor as if there had been no interruption, resuming the complicated hiding and

47

exploring games they had invented around the garden, out of her mother's sight. But Conor must be eighteen now, no longer the gardener's boy but a young man with his own way to make in life. His way and hers would inevitably be very different. And he had already faced a bitter loss.

She said slowly, "I'm sorry about Fergal."

His expression changed and he looked down at the ground and kicked at a stone embedded in the path. "Yes. I'm sorry too."

For a few moments neither spoke, both looking down at the scuffed toe of his boot as he finally kicked the stone free and sent it ricocheting against a birch trunk. Catherine, wanting to say more, could think of nothing to add that wasn't either inquisitive or an empty platitude.

Conor looked up at her. "Your brother came back, anyway."

His voice had a hard edge to it which was unfamiliar to her. And then he seemed to realise that he had spoken harshly, and his voice softened. "Ah, it's not your fault. It's the way of the world. That much I've learned." One hand caressed the soft fur of the rabbits. "Well, I must be getting these home before there are folk about."

"I'm glad I saw you. I hope we – will you be here again?"

He raised his eyebrows. "You won't be after putting your dad on to me now?"

"I said I wouldn't."

"You did. But – Miss Catherine – you really oughtn't to be walking about on your own like this."

"I'm not on my own now that I've met you. And you never called me Miss Catherine before. Caitlin. You used to call me Caitlin."

"Things have moved on since then. You must know that." He looked at her closely for a moment, almost puzzled. If he smiled now he would become the lively boy she remembered, and their relationship would be as it had been.

He did smile, but in such a tight-lipped, half-regretful way that it hardly seemed a smile at all.

"All right, Caitlin then. I'm here often enough, if you want to find me. But be careful."

At breakfast, Andrew said that he was taking the car into Dublin for the day, and his step-mother promptly suggested that Catherine should go with him.

"You really need some new things, my darling. Call in at the dressmaker's and get yourself measured for a new evening dress and a couple for daytime. She'll put it down to my account and send the things on when they're ready."

"Thank you, but – " Catherine felt sure that

Andrew would not want to be saddled with her for a whole day. But once her mother had made up her mind, other people's views were simply swept aside.

"You can have a lovely day together," Delia said.

Catherine wanted to wait and see how Martin was; there had been no sign of him this morning. Andrew, who was in army uniform today, looked equally displeased at having arrangements made for him. "I've an interview at the Castle to see about my new appointment. I'm not sure how long I shall be," he pointed out. "Catherine would have to wait around for me."

"Nonsense, darling. I've a number of errands for her. She'll have plenty to keep her busy. She'd only be bored here."

Paddy Kerrigan brought the car round to the front door after breakfast and Andrew got into the driving seat. Catherine tied her hat down with a large veil, and her mother handed her a list of instructions so long that she wondered whether she would have any time left to herself at all.

"The cakes must be from *Bewley's*, remember. Nowhere else will do."

The hood was down, and Andrew had put on goggles, so that his face when he turned to speak to Catherine reminded her of some enormous insect.

"I didn't really mind bringing you, you know," he shouted as he steered the car out through the wrought-iron gates. "It's just that I'm not sure how long I shall be this morning, and I've got someone else to see this afternoon. If I can get away in time I'll take you to lunch at the Shelbourne."

The noise of the engine combined with the wind in their faces to make prolonged conversation difficult. After exchanging a few remarks they lapsed into silence and Catherine looked out at the soft swell of the Wicklow Hills rising to a sky striated with floating streamers of cloud. In the villages they passed through, ragged children stared at the motor car, and as the car climbed higher she saw a donkey standing patiently by the roadside while a turf-cutter bent over the neat dark trenches, digging stripes into the hillside. What would it be like to spend all day digging in the hot sun, she wondered, and then to go home to a smoky cottage, probably without running water, or enough to eat? What would the turf-cutter think if he were suddenly whisked off to Dublin to have smart clothes made and buy cream cakes at Bewley's and have lunch at the Shelbourne? Flying to the moon could hardly seem a remoter prospect.

And then, thinking of Conor, she wondered what the Kerrigans' cottage in the village was like. Previously, they had lived in the gardener's cottage at Mullaghcleevaun, but for some reason they had moved out two years ago, and now Paddy cycled up to the house each day. Catherine had never visited their cottage. There was no woman in the family, Conor's mother having died when he was quite young. How did the two men provide for themselves? She pictured Conor coming home from the forge with his back aching from bending and lifting horses' hooves all day, having to skin and stew the rabbits he had caught earlier before he could have anything to eat.

It occurred to her that she knew very little about all the lives going on around her, lives on which her own comfort depended. What was the point of her expensive education, of going away to Switzerland to learn how to descend a staircase decorously or how to address a letter to an archbishop, if you knew nothing about people and how they lived? Her knowledge of people began and ended with her family and her school, and her own half-brother had become almost a stranger to her since he had joined the army. Andrew called her little sister, and took her out in the car, but how well did she really know him?

Today might be a good chance to find out more, she thought.

After a morning spent in her shift while her mother's dressmaker took measurements and held swathes of fabric against her to show how they would drape, Catherine met Andrew outside Trinity College and they walked down Grafton Street to the Shelbourne Hotel. Andrew's was not the only uniform to be seen in the crowded thoroughfare; there were British army regulars, privates, who saluted Andrew as they passed, and other troops in a uniform Catherine had not seen before, a strange combination of dark jacket and khaki trousers. She supposed that these must be the "Black and Tans" Maura had spoken about, English reinforcements for the police. A troop lorry made its way along one of the streets bordering St. Stephen's Green and a passer-by shouted something at it; Catherine could not catch the words, but the hostility in the man's voice was plain enough. She sensed a curious air of tension in the streets, as if something out of the ordinary were about to happen; but Andrew made no comment, and led the way into the hotel, where they were greeted by a liveried doorman.

The restaurant was discreetly elegant. She felt very grown-up, almost sophisticated, as they were shown to a table for two by an attentive *maître d'hôtel*. Andrew let her choose what she wanted from the menu instead of advising her as her mother would have done, and he ordered wine with the meal and poured her a glass without asking whether she wanted any. She was pleased that he was treating her as if she were a friend of his own age rather than his schoolgirl sister. She could pretend that she were a glamorous young woman-about-town being taken for lunch by an admirer. Perhaps, to other people in the restaurant, that was what she and Andrew looked like.

She tried to dismiss thoughts of Conor and his rabbit stew from her conscience while she embarked on oxtail soup and tender lamb cutlets with delicately seasoned vegetables. She thought instead of home, and wondered whether Martin would have felt well enough to get up for lunch. Her meeting with Conor had ousted Martin from her thoughts and she realised with a pang of guilt that she had hardly thought about him since leaving home.

"Do you think Martin will be all right?" she asked Andrew.

Andrew continued to eat for a few moments before replying and then said, "I'm not sure what's supposed to be the matter with him. He seems perfectly normal for most of the time."

"Did he have a terrible time in the war?"

"I've never discussed it with him," Andrew replied shortly. "I don't see that his war could have been more unpleasant than anybody else's. It wasn't exactly a picnic."

"Was it horrible, being in the war?"

Andrew looked at her tolerantly, holding his knife and fork poised above his plate. "It was a job that had to be done. As I said, not a very pleasant one. But it's over now and life goes on. For most of us," he added pointedly, and resumed eating.

Catherine felt hurt by his lack of sympathy. "You saw Martin last night at dinner. Obviously he couldn't help himself – he was in a state of collapse. You can't blame him for that."

"I've said nothing to imply that I blame him for anything. I imagine his condition would be diagnosed as shell-shock these days. I've seen plenty of fellows like it. In the front line they either got control of themselves or they reported sick and managed to get themselves out of danger."

"It's not fair to say that," Catherine retorted, "not when you say yourself you've never even talked to him about it. You've got no imagination."

"And you, little sister, seem to have too much."

His amused tone infuriated her. "Besides, he didn't get himself out of danger, did he? He stayed in the army right to the end. You're not being fair at all."

"All right, all right," Andrew said in tones of exasperated reasonableness. "I wasn't talking about Martin in particular – just telling you what I saw when I was out there. Now let's talk about something else. Did you order your dresses?"

"Yes, thank you," Catherine said. She did not want to talk about dresses. "Tell me about your new job," she ventured instead. "Is it a promotion?"

Andrew's closed expression suggested that this was equally unwelcome as a topic of conversation, but he answered, "Not exactly. It's a special unit of the army that's being set up."

Catherine was surprised. "But why? The war's over, isn't it? I thought the army was getting rid of men, not appointing more."

"The war in Europe may be over. There's another kind of war going on here, though."

"You mean here in Ireland? You think there's going to be civil war?"

He fiddled impatiently with his napkin. "Catherine, you can't be so obtuse that you haven't noticed. What did you think last night's little incident was all about?"

"I know that, but – I didn't know it was a war." Her idea of war involved trenches and tanks and marching soldiers in khaki, and it happened somewhere else.

"Of a kind."

"So your new job is to stop things like last night's shootings?"

He grimaced. "Shh, Catherine. There's no need to advertise it to the whole dining room. But yes, to try to stop things like that."

"Isn't that dangerous? You might be shot yourself, like that RIC man last night."

"Anything's dangerous. But you needn't worry. Mine is mainly an administrative role."

She looked down at her empty plate. Administrative. That meant organising things, keeping papers and accounts. That didn't sound too risky. But he had called it war, all the same. She remembered what Patsy had said, about Irishmen dying in an English war. At least in that war you had known who was on which side. Here, it was more difficult. Her parents, and people who visited the house, tended to speak of the Shinners as if they were some faceless menace, or, more often, a disorganised bunch of hooligans. But the Sinn Feiners did have faces. They were not some anonymous entity, but people: people who wanted independence for their country.

"Wouldn't it be easier if Ireland did have Home Rule?" she asked. "Then there wouldn't be any shootings and you wouldn't need to have a special army unit to keep the peace."

Andrew laughed, summoning the waiter for the next course. "That rabble couldn't run the country for five minutes. They'd bring us all to ruin and then have no choice but to turn to the English government for help. Can you imagine it? Besides, Home Rule wouldn't be enough for them now, not after that business back in '16. They want complete independence from England."

The waiter came and took the orders for dessert. When he had gone, Catherine said, "I don't see why Ireland shouldn't at least have the chance to govern itself."

Andrew looked at her through narrowed eyes. "I'd be very careful about repeating notions you've picked up from that opinionated friend of yours. Maura doesn't seem to understand that it's different for people of our class. We've too much to lose."

"We're Irish, aren't we?"

"We're Anglo-Irish, Catherine. It's an important distinction. Doesn't it occur to you that our own position would be a difficult one in an independent Ireland – as landowners of English descent? And, by the way, I'd be grateful if you didn't mention what I've just told you in front of the servants. It's more complicated than you think. You're too young to understand."

The waiter brought her lemon pudding and she ate it sulkily, feeling like a child again.

Filtered light on Martin's eyelids made him groan and stir. Oh, God. Morning. He should have been ready and out there ages ago. That useless servant was meant to have woken him with his tea and shaving-water in good time. This would mean another wigging from the captain, and he could already picture the smugly contemptuous look he would get from the new second lieutenant, the captain's blue-eyed boy . . .

And then he opened his eyes and the room came slowly into focus, and he saw that the curtain through which the light filtered was not a piece of tattered sacking but a Liberty print, and that instead of lying fully dressed on a hard bunk covered with a horse-blanket, he was wearing silk pyjamas and lay between starched sheets. He was not in the Ypres salient but in Ireland, and it was summer. Outside, a turtle-dove was crooning, and he could hear voices on the lawn, the colonel's and Delia's.

He ought to have felt relief, but something nagged at the edges of his consciousness, something he could not shake off. He remembered that he'd made a fool of himself at the dinner table – why? what had made him go off his head like that? – and he dimly remembered faces angled up at him like a row of skulls strung round the room, staring from blank eye-sockets ... And then Andrew giving instructions, the girl's hands gentle at his throat as she removed his bow tie and unfastened his collar studs ... He had somehow got up to his room and had swallowed some pills, and Andrew had got him into bed, and then he remembered no more.

But it was some other memory which lay heavy on him like a physical feeling of sickness in the pit of his stomach. He realised that he had had the dream again, the dream which went on and on, waiting until the screen of his mind was cleared of the flickering impressions of daytime events to replay itself like a cinema film shown again and again ...

He could smell the cordite and the sweat from sodden khaki, and the odour of corruption, of dead flesh, which hung over the trenches from countless bodies rotting in no-man's-land or half-buried in the parapet. The foulness filled his lungs with every sobbing breath. He was running, or trying to run, through mud as clinging as quicksand, so that his legs were pulled down with each step. He didn't know where he was running to, or whether he was in fact running away from something, but the sense of urgency spurred him foward, to some destination always out of sight. He was falling over the legs of dead or dying men, and floundering through shell-holes filled with stinking, stagnant water; the dark sky trembled with great splintering crashes as if it would shatter in pieces and rain down on him and crush him. His legs lost all their strength and he struggled against a weight dragging him down, down into the clayey swirl which rose up to engulf him, drown him, the mud filling his eyes, his nose, his lungs . . .

But he was awake now. He had acknowledged the dream and could send it back to the deep, unreachable part of his mind where it would lie, dormant but unerasable, until the next time.

He picked up his watch from the bedside table and saw that it was half-past two in the afternoon.

Conversation in the Rose Walk

"Do I have to go?" Catherine said grumpily. She couldn't see the point of having lunch with the Fitzwilliams; they'd seen them less than a week ago and now they would sit over another lengthy meal and exchange much the same conversation.

"Of course you must," her mother said. "It would look so absurd if you didn't. And it will be nice for you to see Maura again."

Her mother seemed to delight in throwing people together who had no desire for each other's company, Catherine thought resentfully, getting ready. She brushed out her hair and pinned it up, wondering what her parents would say if she had it all cropped off in the new boyish style she'd seen in fashion magazines. She rather wished she had taken the chance in Dublin to have it cut off, to shock them all.

Andrew had gone to the Dublin barracks, so the party consisted of four: the Colonel and Mrs Enright, Catherine and Martin. Catherine thought that Martin was probably as reluctant to go as she was herself, after his dramatic exit on the previous occasion. But he looked better today, and complimented her on her appearance.

"It's good to see you looking so much recovered, Mr Sheringham," Mrs Fitzwilliam greeted him. "We're so pleased you felt able to come."

"Do come and have a drink on the terrace before lunch." Mr Fitzwilliam spread an expansive arm. Catherine knew that he and her father would spend the afternoon deep in contemplation of flowering shrubs and herbaceous perennials; both were immensely proud of their gardens. The Fitzwilliams' house was grander than Mullaghcleevaun, built of grey stone, with a porticoed front, and Italianate gardens overlooking a wooded valley.

"Now, why don't you show Catherine the rose walk?" Mrs Fitzwilliam suggested to Maura when they had been served with fruit cordial. "It's looking at its best."

"If you wish," Maura said dutifully.

Catherine wished that Mrs Fitzwilliam wouldn't treat them like children. Infuriating though her own mother might be in many ways, she didn't speak to them in quite that patronising manner.

The two girls descended the stone steps from the terrace. Expecting that she and Maura would have little to say to each other, Catherine surveyed the garden. Roses and shrubs bloomed in profusion, interspersed with paved walks and pergolas, Italian statuary and stone benches.

"Here's the rose walk," Maura said.

The borders were thickly planted with roses graduating in colour from white through shades of yellow and peach to deepest pink. Their heady perfume hung warm and fragrant in the air, intoxicating.

"It's beautiful," Catherine said.

"Oh, yes." Maura spoke almost absent-mindedly. "Yes, it's a beautiful garden, and a beautiful house, and we've everything we could wish for. We're very lucky."

"You don't sound very happy about it," Catherine commented.

"No, I suppose I'm not. I probably ought to be grateful – but, well, don't you sometimes feel it's all a bit pointless?"

"What do you mean?"

"I mean – don't you think there are more important things to do than have meals at each other's houses and wear nice clothes and stroll about gardens? What's it all for?"

"I don't know." Catherine was surprised by the suddenness of this outburst. Even though she had been thinking something very similar herself earlier in the morning, she could think of no reply. Maura did not usually ask for her opinion.

"It's as if we have to fill our lives with picnics and parties and dinners," Maura said, "because we're afraid of stopping. We might find that we've left ourselves nothing else to do."

"What would you rather be doing?"

Maura sat down on a stone bench and motioned Catherine to sit beside her. "Something better – I don't really know, either – something with a purpose. Our lives are so narrow. It's as if families like ours feel we have to stick together, to pretend ours is the only way of life that matters."

Catherine stared at her. Andrew had said something rather similar the other day at lunch. But Maura was disagreeing with Andrew's point of view, saying something different altogether.

"Have you thought, for example," Maura went on, "how many people's lives are taken up with looking after us – cooking our food and cleaning our houses and weeding our gardens – working hard so that we can have comfortable lives and never have to lift a finger for ourselves? How many servants are there at Mullaghcleevaun?"

"Well – " Catherine had to think before replying. There was Patsy, and Paddy Kerrigan, and Bridie; and she had an idea that there was a woman from the village who came in to do the laundry. "Three or four, I think."

"There, you don't even know. We've got five – five servants for three of us. And what's it all for? What's the future for you and me? What will you do, for example, when you leave school?"

Catherine, surprised by Maura's unusual animation, felt for the first time a bond of sympathy with her, although she did not know how to express it. Maura's ideas echoed her own train of thought about the turf-cutter on the road to Dublin. At the same time she felt a little out of her depth, because what Maura was saying sounded like Socialism. She had never suspected that Maura might be a Socialist. She knew that Maura was one of a small, earnest group who went for extra lessons and discussions with a young history mistress, Miss Samuels, who had been a member of the Women's Social and Political Union, and provided them with all sorts of reading matter. Catherine had an idea that Miss Samuels and her group were not approved of by the headmistress. To Catherine's less serious-minded circle of friends, Maura and her peers were considered rather odd. And yet Maura had come closer than anyone else to sympathising with her own doubts about their way of life.

"I shall spend one more year at school and

after that Mother wants me to go to a finishing school in Switzerland," she replied.

"Exactly." Maura sounded triumphant. "And what's the aim of that? So that you can get yourself a husband and a big house, and know how to manage the servants and give smart dinner parties. It goes on, you see."

"Don't you want to get married? I think I do."

"That's not the point. Yes, I might like to get married if I meet the right person, but what if I don't? That shouldn't be my only choice, should it?"

Catherine found herself wondering, rather unkindly, whether Maura's ideas stemmed from a doubt that she would make a successful marriage. No one could possibly describe Maura as attractive. She was tall for a girl, with long limbs which gave her a certain awkwardness of movement. Her face was too thin and angular, her hair a nondescript brown and of the thin, wiry sort which would not adapt easily to any sort of style. She was the sort of girl who didn't get invited to dance, and had to sit at the side of ballrooms pretending to enjoy herself. Perhaps she was pretending to dislike men and marriage as a sort of protection, Catherine thought. But she could see that Maura's point was a valid one – why should she submit to being groomed for marriage, if she didn't want it?

"There's been a war fought and women have done all sorts of essential work in it, and yet as far as our families are concerned, nothing's changed at all!" Maura continued. "We're to grow up as accomplished young ladies – accomplished in all sorts of useless ways, that is. I wish I'd been born a boy."

"Oh, I don't. You might have had to fight in the war, and – "

"And have a proper education, and have some choice of a career," Maura finished for her. "What sort of education did your brother have?"

"He went to school in England and then to Oxford University."

"Quite," Maura said crisply.

"What do you mean, quite?"

"For instance, has it ever been suggested that you go to university? Women can, you know."

"I'm not clever enough."

"Well, I am." Maura stated it as a fact, not making it a boast. "But have you ever heard of anyone going to a university from Kingswood House?"

Catherine had never thought about it. "I don't think many of the girls want to, do they?"

"Probably not. It's not that kind of school. It's a school for turning out quiet, docile young ladies. *Marriageable* young ladies."

"I see what you mean," Catherine said. "It doesn't seem fair, what you say about choices, especially for someone as ambitious as you are. But I think I do want to get married, really."

"Oh, all right," Maura said wearily.

Catherine felt that she had let herself down. Maura seemed to have given up, and was looking away, towards the house. Catherine followed her gaze and saw Martin standing by a fountain higher up the lawn, looking towards them. Catherine hoped that he would come and join them; it would be interesting to hear his views on what they had been discussing.

"You might as well marry your cousin, in that case," Maura remarked. "He's very good-looking, isn't he? Can cousins marry?"

"I don't know. But actually we're not blood relations at all. He's really Andrew's cousin, not mine. Martin's mother was the sister of my father's first wife."

"That's all right, then," Maura said, as if the matter were settled.

Arrest

Daylight was fading from the village street. Most of the inhabitants were indoors resting or having their evening meal; the road was quiet apart from a pair of children playing a game with stones and a stick. A chicken pecked in the dust and a thin black dog slunk from doorway to doorway, occasionally shooed away roughly.

The Crossley tender passed into the village almost unnoticed. The driver pulled up by a whitewashed cottage at the end of the street, and five men in dark tunics and khaki trousers jumped to the ground. One of them hammered abruptly on the cottage door, which after a few moments opened fractionally to reveal the frightened face of a girl of ten or so.

"Is your father in?" the sergeant demanded in an English accent. "Police."

The girl backed away in alarm. The sergeant pushed the door fully open and went in, followed by two of his companions, while the driver stayed with the vehicle and two other men kept guard by the front door.

Inside, a small peat fire smouldered in the hearth, over which hung a crucifix. The English sergeant cast an indifferent glance around the room, which was inhabited by a thin dark-haired woman, two other children and a baby as well as the girl who had opened the door, and a man in his thirties who rose slowly from a rocking chair by the hearth.

"Liam Mulcahy. You're to be taken into custody," the officer said.

The two constables behind him had revolvers cocked.

The woman let out a wail. "He's done nothing! You shan't take him, I tell you!"

The sergeant spared her a brief glance, but did not answer.

"Amn't I telling you he's done nothing!" the woman repeated, her voice rising hysterically.

Her husband, seeming to ignore her, pulled on a tweed jacket and prepared to leave calmly with the sergeant. She grabbed at his arm, shouting incoherently. The man simply pushed her away, gently but firmly, looked at the faces of his children and walked out of the door, given a rough push from behind. The last constable to leave slammed the door hard, and the baby's voice rose in a thin quavering wail.

The prisoner's wife wrenched the door open.

Finding her voice again, she screamed after the tender as the driver steered away from the cottage. "He's innocent, I'm telling you! Leave us in peace, you murthering swine!" And then she burst into angry tears, with the two smaller children clutching at her skirt.

Other villagers had come out into the street to see what was happening, and the black dog took advantage of the disturbance to sneak through an open door and eat a plateful of stew from a kitchen table.

Oystercatchers

"You might be seeing something of your old friend around the place," the colonel remarked to Catherine over breakfast.

"What old friend?"

"Young Conor Kerrigan. I've hired him to do some odd jobs for me while the light evenings last."

"Oh," Catherine said. She was sure she was blushing, not wanting to let slip that she'd seen Conor already. She bent over the marmalade pot and concentrated on extracting a piece of peel with the spoon.

"Yes, I'm getting him to clean out the gardener's cottage. And when he's done that I'll get him on to scrub clearance in the woods," her father went on, not noticing. "He's a good lad, Conor. Trustworthy."

Martin, however, was looking at Catherine with interest across the table. She caught his eye and was furious to feel her cheeks growing hotter still.

"I'm thinking of getting a new gardener, if I can find anyone suitable. It's all getting a bit much for Paddy – he's finding the general repair work more than enough." The colonel sighed. "The old house isn't what it was . . . Before the war I used to employ two full-time gardeners and a boy. Of course we used to grow a lot more of our own produce then."

"Yes, I remember," Martin said. "Peaches from the conservatory. Delicious."

"If we get a new gardener we could have them again," the Colonel said. "Ah well, I must get on . . . things to do . . . Now how are you two young people going to occupy yourselves today?"

Delia had woken up with a slight headache and was taking breakfast in her room. Catherine felt her absence as something of a relief; one of her mother's main priorities was seeing that everyone else's day was organised for them. She thought of the unexpected freedom, hours stretching in front of her to be filled as she wished.

Martin said, "I thought, if you didn't mind, Uncle Douglas, I might take Catherine down to the coast."

"Excellent idea. Make the most of the fine weather . . . you'll need the car, then. I won't be wanting it today, neither will Delia . . . I'll tell

Kerrigan to bring it round for you."

"That's very kind of you, Uncle," Martin said, rising politely to his feet as the colonel left the room. Then he sat down again and looked at Catherine. "I should have asked you first if you wanted to go. You don't mind, do you?"

Her mouth was full of toast. She swallowed it as quickly as she could and said, "Of course not. I'd love to."

"I wonder if we could take a picnic – make a day of it?"

"I'll ask Patsy to pack us a basket. She won't mind."

The arrangements were made, and the car brought round. Catherine settled herself in the passenger seat, and Martin passed her a folded map.

"Here. I don't know if we'll need this, but I'm in your hands."

Martin drove more carefully than Andrew, deferring to Catherine for directions. She took them down through the village and on to the main road which led to the coast. In Fanagmore, two young women in shawls turned and looked at the car and its occupants in a way which struck Catherine as hostile. She thought Martin hadn't noticed, but after a few moments he said, "I suppose we're lucky there's been so little trouble around here, when you read of what's happening in other parts of the country."

"Yes. It's easy for us to ignore it. We lead such enclosed lives – " she found herself echoing what Maura had said the day before " – that we can pretend nothing's going on." But for the first time she felt uneasy, seeing herself for a moment as the village women must see her – a representative of inherited wealth and privilege in a country to which she did not really belong.

This uncomfortable thought was soon displaced by the anticipated pleasure of spending a whole day with Martin. She kept thinking of Maura's remark, that she might as well marry him. Maura had not been serious, but was it possible that Martin could forget the age difference and his broken engagement, and think of her in that way? Not now, of course, she really was too young, but in a year or two, perhaps, when she had left school . . . Juliet was fourteen, she thought, nearly two years younger than me; and Shakespeare didn't treat her as a silly child, did he, for loving Romeo? It was her parents who were the foolish ones . . .

They drove down the coastal road, leaving the car where a sandy track petered out at the edge of the dunes, and walked through marram grass and soft pale sand which spilled into their shoes. There was a light wind. The patterns of sunlight were changing, shifting over the sea so that its depths seemed first to reflect back blue sky and then to contain vivid green shadows. The tide was low and a line of oystercatchers stood by the sea's edge; most were immobile but one or two stalked the sand in agitation, shrieking their shrill cry which always made Catherine think that some disaster was at hand.

"They're like birds drawn by a child with a paintbox," she said to Martin, "great black and white patches, gaudy orange for the bill and legs. They're like clowns. Clowns of the seashore."

"What are they called?"

"Oystercatchers."

"Do they catch oysters?"

"Yes, of course. Well, shellfish anyway. They dig in the sand for them, with their beaks." She was surprised by his lack of knowledge, before realising that he had spent most of his life in London.

"I didn't know you were an ornithologist," he said.

"I'm not. I only know the common birds, the ones around the garden and woods and seashore."

It was Conor who had taught her. He had shown her pictures in an old book he treasured, browning at the edges and fingermarked, and he had taught her to recognise woodland birds by their call. Once in London she had had the idea

77

of getting him a newer bird book, but she had never got around to making the purchase and had forgotten the idea.

"Let's paddle," she suggested. "The tide's too low to swim. Are you going to swim later?"

He shook his head decisively. "No. Swimming's not for me. I might drown."

"You used to like swimming."

"Not any more."

"And anyway I could save you if you looked like drowning. I'm quite a good swimmer."

"I'd rather not give you the chance, thanks all the same."

Martin sat down on the dunes to remove his shoes and socks and Catherine turned away from him to take off her stockings. She shook out sand and folded the stockings in her shoes. Martin rolled up his trousers to the knee. His feet were very pale, with ridges of delicate bone fanning out to the toes, and the calves of his legs were shapely and muscular, shaded with dark hair. She glanced away quickly in case he saw her looking, and put her white shoes neatly side by side in the sand.

"Come on, then," he said, standing up.

They ran down to the water's edge. The oystercatchers flew away with shrill cries, the black and white of their plumage edging into new patterns like shapes in a kaleidoscope as they wheeled against the brightness of the sea. Catherine splashed ahead of Martin into the shallows, sending cold droplets spraying into her face and over her dress. As the drag of the water slowed her quick dash, he caught up with her, grabbing her arm and turning her.

"You might carry on walking into the water and never be seen again. You might turn into a mermaid or a water-sprite."

"And lure sailors to their doom?"

"It'd be doom for me all right if I had to go home without you and explain that you'd taken to a life in the sea."

"You could come and visit me here in secret and I could sit on a rock and play you bewitching songs on my harp of gold," Catherine suggested. "But I'd be a bit too plump for a mermaid, and aren't they supposed to have long golden hair and sea-green eyes?"

Conor has green eyes, she thought: eyes whose colour shifts and changes like the sea.

"I'd settle for a plump dark-haired mermaid to sing me songs."

They giggled at the idea, and began to walk along the shoreline through small frills of wavelets.

"Tell me," Martin said, "about Conor."

"What about Conor?" Catherine said, taken aback. Had he read her thoughts just now? "You mean what Father said at breakfast? That's all I know."

"I mean, why did you blush when his name was mentioned? I suspect romantic interest."

"Between me and Conor? Of course not. It wouldn't be seemly for me to have a romantic interest in the gardener's boy, would it?" she said in her mother's voice. "I haven't seen him for a long while. If I blushed it was probably because it'll be strange to see him after so long. That's all."

Martin looked sceptical, but said nothing.

"Oh, all right then," she said. "It was because I *have* seen Conor. I met him by chance, in the woods."

"Aha! A romantic tryst! I suspected as much. Sherlock Sheringham, super-sleuth, is hot on the trail."

"Well, Sherlock Sheringham has got it wrong. And if we're going to talk about romance, why don't you tell me about Serena?"

Oh, God, she thought. Why had she come out with it as bluntly as that? She had meant to lead up to it gradually. Now he would be offended and their day would be spoiled. Or suppose he collapsed again in one of his turns? How would she manage then?

Martin looked away from her out to sea, his eyes narrowed. He walked more slowly, trailing his feet in the lapping waves.

"Martin, I'm sorry," she said, alarmed at her crassness. "I didn't mean to ask straight out like that. You don't have to answer."

"It's all right," he said slowly. "Serena. Well. You never met her, did you?"

She shook her head.

"I first met her at a party in London. Once on leave I went up to her family's country place, in Shropshire, and then we met up a few more times in London. It was one of those wartime engagements, you know the sort of thing: you might be dead tomorrow, so make the most of today . . . I thought she was the most marvellous girl. Pretty, amusing, friendly. And the amazing thing was that she took to me straight away, too."

"That isn't amazing," Catherine said, but Martin appeared not to have heard, and continued.

"We wrote to each other all the time. I had her photograph with me in the trenches. I've still got it, as a matter of fact. All the time I was out there I thought of getting back to her – finishing with the army as soon as I could so that I could go home and marry her. I was still thinking that, even while I was crossing the Channel for the last time, from Rouen . . . counting the hours till I'd see her. And then, the day I was actually going to see her at last, I woke up and knew I couldn't go through with it."

Their feet rhythmically threshed the water, waves rippling their ankles. Catherine said, "But why not? Surely you deserved to be happy, after all you'd done in the war? Didn't you love her after all?"

"It's hard to explain. It's . . . I felt stained, dirty. I knew I'd never be the same again. I thought . . . I'm not good enough for her, never can be. I'll never be clean again. I felt dirty, right through."

Trying to understand, Catherine said, "You mean – because you had to kill people, kill Germans? Is that what you mean by feeling dirty?"

Martin said nothing for a few moments, pressing his lips tightly together. It seemed to Catherine that he feared letting out too many words if he opened them. Then he said, "It . . . it was one thing . . . one time in particular. It nearly finished me. But I had to do it. I had to obey orders or I'd have been in the same boat myself. Do you know what they did to . . . to deserters, or people who . . . showed cowardice, as they called it? Do you know what happened to them?"

"They were punished, I suppose," Catherine said.

Martin laughed humourlessly. "Punished, yes.

Sometimes they were . . . they were shot . . . executed. As an example to the others. It was meant to stiffen the morale of the troops. Nice euphemism, that . . . it means scare them stupid, so they'll do anything they're ordered. Well, we were up in the salient, around Ypres . . . a ghastly place, a stinking swamp, littered with dead men and horses by the time I got there . . . you thought you'd never get out again, you'd rot there . . . We were in an advance, told to capture some wood or other. You can't imagine how impossible it was. They'd give you a neat plan showing roads and farms and villages. Then you'd look at where you were supposed to go and it was a morass of mud with the odd tree-stump or pile of rubble poking above it . . . You'd advance in the dark with no idea whether you were going the right way or not. Well, this time a man in my platoon – a boy called Panton, only nineteen – he must have got lost, because next day when we . . . when those of us who were left . . . were trying to hang on, just a matter of yards further on from where we'd started, he was picked up by military police . . . and next day he was hauled up for a court martial."

"And they shot him?" Catherine was appalled. "For getting lost?"

Martin nodded. "I haven't got to the worst

part yet . . . Someone had to command the firing-squad . . . and the someone was me."

Catherine stared at him. "That's horrible. They made you do that?"

"Yes . . . Captain Waverley – he was the company commander – disliked me for some reason . . . That's why he made me do it. He knew, and so did I, that if I refused I'd be up for a court martial myself, for defying orders. He . . . Panton . . . he was very brave. He held his head up, didn't plead for mercy the way I've heard some prisoners did . . . He didn't say anything at all. They led him out and blindfolded him and tied him to a chair. The firing-squad was made up of men from my platoon . . . you can imagine how they felt, under orders to shoot their own mate . . . but the only decent thing is to get it over with as soon as possible, shoot straight . . . it'd only be worse for the poor blighter if they didn't . . . So I had to give the command, Ready, aim, fire – " Martin had stopped walking and stood tensed as if giving instruction to soldiers who stood beside him, rifles aimed. "My job was to have a revolver handy so that I could finish off the poor beggar with a bullet through the head if by any chance he was still alive . . . but he was dead, the chair had toppled over and he was on the ground still tied to it, riddled with bullets. I was glad it was over quickly for him ... I'd seen men killed before, dozens of them, at the front ... but this was the most callous, cold-blooded thing I ever saw. And I'd had to do it myself."

His voice had dropped to a whisper and he stood gazing sightlessly at the curve of coastline. Ahead, the oystercatchers by the tide's edge probed the wet sand.

Warnings

"I'm sorry," Martin said as they walked back slowly through the dunes. "I wanted to bring you out for a pleasant day by the sea. It wasn't fair of me to burden you with all that."

"I asked, didn't I?" Catherine said. "And I'm glad you did tell me. I understand now why you reacted like that the other night . . . why you're upset sometimes. Anyone would be. But it really wasn't your fault. You mustn't blame yourself for what happened."

"Ah well." Martin shrugged, seeming to close the subject. "Now we're going to forget all about the war. We're going to be day trippers and explore rock pools and picnic in the dunes and enjoy ourselves."

By the time they left for home, late in the afternoon, the sky had clouded over, although there was still enough warmth in the air to make it unnecessary to wear coats for the journey. They drove back in companionable silence. Inside the gates of Mullaghcleevaun House,

Martin brought the car to a standstill outside the porch and turned off the ignition. Then he said, "I've enjoyed our day, enjoyed it enormously. Thank you," and he leaned across and kissed her on the cheek.

Pleased, she said, "Don't thank me. It was your idea." She would have liked to kiss him back, but her attention was diverted by a tall figure standing in the open doorway of the gardener's cottage, cigarette in hand. Conor. He raised the cigarette to his lips and looked straight towards the car, but made no acknowledgement of having seen her. She felt unaccountably guilty at the thought that he must have seen Martin kissing her.

"Come on," she said, "let's go inside and see if we're too late for tea. All that sea air's made me hungry again."

The Enrights and Martin attended the Sunday morning church service. Afterwards, as usual, the Protestant families of the area gathered outside in knots to exchange conversation and news. Catherine, bored, looked at moss-encrusted gravestones and listened idly to a conversation between her mother and Mr Lewknor, who bred horses.

"So your son's gone back to Dublin now, Mrs Enright?"

"Yes, he took up his new post on Thursday."

"It's for the best, I'm thinking, with these gunmen round about. You probably felt it a risk having him at home, the way things are."

Catherine had her back to her speakers but she could hear the offended inhalation of breath before her mother replied.

"I assure you, Mr Lewknor, that such a thought never entered my head, nor my husband's. Apart from the incident last week there hasn't been a hint of trouble in these parts."

"Ah, well now. I wonder did you know a man's been arrested for that shooting? A man from Lisgarvan, so I heard."

"I really didn't interest myself much in the matter, Mr Lewknor. I assumed that it would be dealt with by the police. And if what you say is correct then it seems that they've dealt with it expeditiously."

At that point, Maura, who had been standing with her parents beneath the holm oak talking to the minister, detached herself and came over to Catherine. "I must tell you – " She slipped her arm through Catherine's and drew her a little apart from the rest of the congregation.

"Tell me what?"

"The Black and Tans have taken a man to barracks and executed him for the murder of that RIC sergeant."

"Executed!" Catherine thought of the rifles lined up, the condemned man tied to a chair, the commander of the firing-squad giving the order; the scene was vivid in her mind since Martin had described it to her. "Who told you that?"

"One of our maids has a brother who delivers fish and he heard it in Lisgarvan. Isn't it terrible?"

"Well, if he was guilty of murder . . . That would be justice, surely?"

"The point is," Maura said, "that no one bothered to find out whether he was guilty or not. He was executed without a trial."

"You mean . . . just like in the war, soldiers being shot as an example to others?"

"It wasn't justice. It was revenge. They had to get someone. And don't you see what this will mean?"

"What?"

But before Maura could say more, Catherine felt a hand on her shoulder and her mother said, "Maura, how nice. You must come over to tea one day soon and keep Catherine company. Now do tell me where you found that delightful hat. One like it would just suit Catherine."

When Catherine rose from the table after lunch, her mother put a restraining hand on her arm.

"Darling, don't disappear. I'd like to have a little talk."

This was nearly always a euphemism for a telling-off. Wondering what she had done wrong, Catherine followed her mother into the small chintz sitting room. Delia settled herself on the cushioned sofa and spread out her skirts so that they wouldn't crease, before beginning delicately, "I really felt I ought to warn you, darling, to be careful where Martin's concerned. I know he's a very personable young man and I'm sure his attentions are flattering to you. It's perfectly understandable. But do remember that he's been ill and that he's only recently broken off an engagement. I would so hate you to be disappointed."

Her blue eyes gazed at Catherine with the wide-eyed, concerned expression she used for gentle persuasion. Catherine stooped to bury her face in the yellow roses on the writing-desk, breathing in their musky fragrance.

"I don't know what you mean," she lied. "I don't think of Martin in that way – the way you're implying. There's nothing like that. I thought you wanted me to keep him company?"

"Keep him company, yes. Just remember that's all it is. He's considerably older than you and he has his war trauma to cope with. You can't begin to understand what goes on in his mind – don't delude yourself that you can. You're too young to understand."

Catherine flared back, "I'm sure I understand more than you do. He's talked to me, told me . . . about the war . . ." She paused, not wanting to betray Martin's confidence.

"I see. And what has he told you?"

"Oh – how awful it was. And why do people keep telling me I'm grown up with one breath and then next minute say I'm too young? It isn't fair." She stopped again, aware that she sounded exactly like a petulant child.

Her mother smiled. "I understand, darling. You're at a difficult age. But you won't forget what I've said, will you? Don't go imagining that Martin's in love with you."

"Can I go now?" Catherine said, choosing not to reply.

"Just a moment more. Why don't you come and sit down?" Delia patted the sofa next to her.

Catherine deliberately sat in an armchair on the opposite side of the room.

"The other thing I really ought to mention," her mother continued, "is the matter of Conor Kerrigan. I was a little concerned when your father told me he'd be working here in the evenings. You do understand, don't you, that it's out of the question for you and Conor to be as friendly as you used to be? I blame myself, in a way – I should have stopped you from playing together as children. Your father didn't see any harm in it, but it was rather short-sighted of me. You do see, I hope, that things are very different now that you're a young lady?"

"Oh, I'm a young lady now? A few moments ago I was a child, too young to understand."

"Catherine, I really cannot allow you to speak to me in that truculent manner. If you wish to be treated as an adult then you must learn to discuss things calmly and reasonably."

"Sorry," Catherine mumbled. "But let me get this quite clear. You don't want me to spend too much time with Martin and you don't want me to spend any time at all with Conor. Who *am* I allowed to spend time with?"

Her mother shifted against the cushions. "Well, I'm delighted that you and Maura enjoy each other's company so much. Maura's a very sensible girl. You can invite her here as often as you wish."

"Thank you," Catherine said, with icy politeness.

She let herself out of the room and closed the door with restrained fury. Prominent in her mind was the thought that, if her mother disapproved of her seeing Conor, then she was going to see him again as soon as possible.

The Gardener's Cottage

Catherine glanced back at the house. Her parents were in their room at the opposite end, changing for dinner; they wouldn't see her. Patsy might notice, if she happened to glance out of the kitchen window, but the windows were all steamed up with cooking, and in any case Patsy wouldn't let on even if she did realise where Catherine was going and why.

Having sniffed the roses in the main border for long enough to provide a pretext for her excursion, Catherine turned and picked her way carefully round to the back of the gardener's cottage. Here, the smooth mown lawns of the house gave way to unkempt wilderness. Spires of purple willowherb vied for position with teasels, seeded grasses and strong suckers of elder, whose branches were laden with clusters of unripe berries. There were tall nettles, too, bristling along Catherine's bare forearm, touching the tender skin with needles of pain. She rubbed her arm vigorously, stifling an exclamation of annoyance, and carried on through the long grass towards the back door. She saw that Conor had already scythed a patch clear of long grass; a heap of chopped wood lay stacked by the door, next to a wheelbarrow piled with rubbish – old newspapers, cardboard boxes, and what looked like discarded garments. She walked up the flagged path to the open door and hesitated on the doorstep, listening. Conor was inside; she could hear him moving about upstairs.

The back door opened straight into the main room. Rusted gardening implements were leaning against one wall, and flowerpots of various sizes were stacked next to piles of seed trays and a box containing withered tubers. The cottage had evidently been used as a gardening store since the Kerrigans had moved out. There was nothing else in the room apart from the fireplace, a big box of crockery on the floor, and two wooden shelves fixed to the wall. Conor had kept his few books there as a child, along with his father's gardening encyclopaedia. The room was much smaller than Catherine remembered it, and it was dusty, so that glittering specks danced in a ray of sunlight slanting in from the begrimed window. Ahead of her the wooden stairs led up to the first floor. She decided to go up and find Conor. As she began to mount the stairs she heard the ceiling creak as footsteps crossed the room to her left, and then he was standing on the top landing, bending forward and looking down at her.

"Catherine! I thought I heard someone down there."

He didn't move aside to let her come up. The flicker of pleasure which had crossed his face at first vanished quickly. He was scowling at her, definitely scowling. She was disappointed.

"You shouldn't come over here," he said, more quietly. "Your ma said I wasn't to talk to you. Or perhaps you've come to tell me that as well?"

"Of course not. Mother said that?"

Conor straightened up. "She sent for me, up to the house. Gave me a flaking. I might be forgetting that I'm just a labourer. She felt it best to remind me." He turned away from her and went back into the upstairs room where he had been working.

Catherine followed him. "Oh, Mother is so tactless. You mustn't mind her, Conor. It makes no difference to me."

"Generous of you," Conor said ironically. "Sure, I don't know why you're taking the trouble to come and tell me. I thought you were taken up with your man there. Your English cousin."

He looked out of the window moodily, both

hands spread out on the windowsill. She wished he would turn round so that she could see his expression; his back view looked unapproachable. She gazed rather despairingly at his bunched shoulders beneath the thin cotton shirt, and at the sunburned back of his neck where the hair curled into the nape.

"Martin's been ill," she said. "He's staying with us to recover."

"He looked all right yesterday."

And then he did turn and look at her. There was dirt smeared along his cheekbone and clinging to one eyebrow. She remembered Martin's kiss, and Conor watching, and it flashed into her mind that Conor was jealous. She was ashamed, and flattered, both at once, and felt herself blushing.

She said, "What you saw yesterday – we'd been out to the beach to talk – to talk about the war. He felt better after that. That was all."

"Ah, you don't have to explain to me. And now you'd better leave me to my work. Your father will be thinking I'm wasting my time." Conor moved past her and picked up a soft broom which he had left leaning against the wall. "Shouldn't you be going in for your dinner?"

"I've only to change my dress."

"You'll be getting yourself filthy in here." He started to sweep briskly. "This place hasn't been lived in for two years and more. This used to be my room. I used to look out of my window and see you running across the grass with your long hair streaming."

His tone was more encouraging. Catherine said, "I rememember how we used to help your father with the vegetable garden. I liked that."

There had been neat rows of cabbages and peas, and the beans had twined up to make green tents around stakes, green tents with pennants of scarlet flowers, beneath which she and Conor had crawled on their knees to pick stones out of the beds.

Conor paused, leaning on his broom handle. "Immaculate, he used to keep that plot. Beautiful. You should see it now, all weeds and thistles."

"If Father gets a new gardener, it'll soon be back the way it was."

"No. Never. I said before, you can't go back. The way it was when we were children, we can never have that time back again."

Catherine watched him while he carried on sweeping. She could smell the dust, taste it on her lips.

She said, "We've had the war, I know, but that's over now, and . . ."

"No, it's not. It's not over yet by a long way. You can't hide from that." Conor leaned into the rhythm of his sweeping with far more energy than the task required.

"At least you were too young to fight."

"I'd never fight for the British, old enough or not. If I'd been of age before the war ended I'd still not have fought. Not after what they did to us in '16."

"You mean the rebellion?"

"Of course that's what I mean. The Easter Rising." He had swept a pile of dust into the corner. He straightened and looked around for a dustpan; seeing none, he leaned the broom against the wall, and pushed past Catherine to clatter downstairs.

She followed him more slowly. Her own recollection of Easter 1916 was dim. She had been staying with her Aunt Margaret in London at the time, and all she had known was that there had been some sort of disturbance in Dublin, so that her intended visit home for the remainder of the school holiday had been cancelled, and she had stayed on with her aunt. She remembered hearing Andrew and her father talk about the rebellion later, when Andrew had been home on leave, and she knew that rebel Republicans had tried to take over the centre of the city. "Stabbing the British army in the back," Andrew had called it. "If we'd had any sense we'd have executed the whole damned lot of them, not just the leaders."

She could clearly remember Andrew saying that, one night at dinner, his face flushed with wine and indignation.

"But was it really the fault of the British," she said to Conor, "if they didn't start it?"

"Ah, you don't understand." Conor was rummaging in a wooden box in the main room, his tone exasperated rather than angry.

"I know I don't understand. People are always telling me I don't understand, but they don't tell me what I need to know. How can I understand?" Her voice rose childishly, betraying her again.

"It's simple enough," Conor said, standing up with the dustpan and brush in his hand. "The British had almost given in over Home Rule. Then war broke out and suddenly Home Rule would have to wait. If we wanted it, we were going to have to prove our right to it by sending thousands of Irish to fight for Britain."

"But we didn't have conscription in Ireland, did we?" Catherine seized on one fact she was sure of. "Not like they did in England. People went of their own free will – your brother – "

"Fergal joined the army because he thought it was a war to protect small countries," Conor said. "Belgium, Ireland – what's the difference? They've both got the right to rule themselves, or should have. If he'd lived, Fergal would have wanted that treaty, last year in France, to make Ireland independent as part of the peace settlement. But, no. We're back where we were before, under English rule. Except that my brother's dead, and died fighting for the English. I never had the chance to ask him what he thought about it, carrying on, after the Rising ... how much he even knew about what had happened. If he'd known the truth, he'd have wanted to get out and come home. The trouble is, you can't say, 'I've had enough of your war, Mr Army-Major, thank you very much. I'm after going home.' Once you're in, the army's got you. You don't belong to yourself any more."

Catherine was frightened by the bitterness in his voice. It made him seem so much older than herself.

"Aren't you glad you didn't have to fight?"

"Before the Rising I'd have done the same as Fergal, I suppose. Afterwards, never. Now will you please be letting me get on with my work upstairs."

He stepped towards her where she stood at the bottom of the stairway. In her haste to get out of his way, she moved aside awkwardly and found herself tripping over a stack of flowerpots, losing her balance. Putting out a hand to steady herself, she was too late to stop herself from sinking to the ground, while the clay pots tumbled and rolled around her in a haze of fine red dust.

"Oh, I'm sorry – " she began, reaching out for the two halves of a broken pot. She looked up at him anxiously, thinking he would be angry with her for messing up the room he had tidied. But he was laughing, stretching out a hand to pull her to her feet, brushing cobwebs from the back of her dress.

"Sure, you're as clumsy as ever," he teased. "Maybe they have got a job on their hands after all to turn you into an elegant lady."

She laughed too, relieved by his change of mood. He was still holding her by the arm and picking bits of cobweb out of her hair; his grip was warm and firm. When he had finished he said, "There. That's better. We can't have you going in for your dinner looking like a scarecrow." Then he stroked his hand down the length of her hair and said, "You've beautiful hair, Caitlin. You should never get it cut off, the way modern girls do."

She turned to face him, and saw that his expression was softened, almost tender. For a crazy moment she thought he was going to kiss her, and in confusion she moved away and said, "It's late . . . I must go."

She bent down to pick up the disordered flower-pots, but Conor said, "I'll do that. You get along now."

At the back door she paused and looked back. "You'll be here tomorrow evening?"

"I will," Conor said.

In the Hay Barn

The midday sun beat down fiercely. A man cutting thistles in a meadow eight miles from Mullaghcleevaun threw down his scythe and straightened stiffly, clutching a hand to his aching back. Time for a rest and a bite to eat, he decided. It was too hot for him to be toiling in the fields, at his age.

He raked the cut thistles into a rough pile to be burned later on, when he had finished the field. He had just seen his employer drive his pony and trap along the dirt road towards town, so there was no one to check up on him and discover that he was about to take his midday break early. The only two human beings in sight were O'Leary's two men, Rourke and his boy, mending fences in the fields which belonged to the neighbouring farm. The elderly man, Dillon, walked slowly towards a stone barn in the corner of the field, his feet brushing the sun-browned grass. The barn would provide cool shade and somewhere to rest out of sight for an hour or so.

He pulled open the heavy wooden door, and slipped inside. The air smelled sweetly of recently cut grasses, and the trussed hay provided a comfortable seat. Dillon eased himself down stiffly and pulled a hunk of bread and cheese from one capacious pocket and a small flask from the other. While he ate, his eyes adjusted to the dim greenish light. One side of the barn was used for the storage of hurdles, planks and fencing posts and various outdated implements. Looking idly in that direction, Dillon noticed a clear path through the dust and hayseeds on the stone floor, as if something had recently been dragged along. He followed the trail with his eyes and then stopped chewing to stare in alarm as his glance fell on a large black workman's boot protruding from behind the hurdles.

He rose cautiously to his feet and moved closer, peering behind the wood-stack. Now he could see two boots, with legs attached clad in brown corduroy. The rest of the figure was shadowed and partly hidden, and Dillon's first thought was that some tinker had crept into the barn for a sleep, like himself. But wouldn't the hay have been more comfortable?

A prod at one of the legs produced no response, and Dillon withdrew his hand hastily on feeling the cold rigidity of the limb beneath the corduroy, certain now that this was no sleeping tinker, but a corpse. Glancing edgily around the barn, he began to lift hurdles and fence-posts carefully aside, stacking them against the hay. The lower half of the body was visible now, but the torso and head were still out of sight behind heavy planks of wood, which would take an age to move. Stooping awkwardly, Dillon took hold of both feet, gritted his teeth and pulled as hard as he could. He was surprised by the heavy resistance of the body, but gradually he tugged it out of its hiding place into view. Dillon muttered an oath as he saw the dark patches on the front of the tweed jacket and a glimpse of deeper staining on the pale shirt beneath. Bullet wounds? A stabbing? A cold chill of fear ran down Dillon's spine. This was clearly not an old tinker who had crawled into the barn and died there, but a murder victim . . .

He placed the feet carefully side by side on the ground and crossed himself, bowing his head in a brief silent prayer for the dead man. The face was still hidden, the neck turned awkwardly to one side, a brown cloth cap pulled down partly hiding the features. Dillon didn't care to look at the face more closely. Suddenly the barn seemed a very different place from the quiet retreat it had been a few moments earlier. Almost believing that masked gunmen might burst from the haystack and take him prisoner, he crept out through the door into the sunlight, and stood for a moment wondering which way to go for help. O'Leary's farmhouse was nearer than his own employer's, and it had a telephone . . .

It was many years since he had run, but now he set off in the direction of the neighbouring farm as quickly as his stiff joints and rasping lungs would let him.

Heaven's Gate

Martin was walking in the Mullaghcleevaun garden, thinking about a leave he had spent in Shropshire, the time when he and Serena had spent a day climbing the Wrekin.

It was early June, in 1917, the first time he had been able to spend more than the occasional evening with Serena. The formality of being a guest at her parents' country home in Shropshire was more than compensated for by their willingness to let him spend time alone with her. He had already seen, in London and during his posting in France, that there was a yielding in the strict code of etiquette which had prevailed before the war; women were doing all kinds of war work, and in their off-duty hours they went to parties and dances, and mixed with men with a freedom unheard of in peacetime. He had been pleased to discover that the relaxation of the social code had reached civilian life, too. Before the war, it would not have been thought seemly for a well brought-up girl like Serena to go about unchaperoned with a young man. Now, her parents waved them off quite happily to spend most of a day together. It was as if his uniform and his role as a junior officer provided a guarantee of respectability. Propriety seemed less important when a few days or hours of leave were all that could be hoped for, and no one knew when the next chance for a meeting would occur.

The sun was shining and there were five clear days of leave ahead, and life seemed good to Martin. He felt fit and healthy from his army training; although his brief spell in France had not yet taken him to the front line, he found himself treated with as much admiration by Serena and her family as if he had returned hung with medals for conspicuous gallantry. He was "Serena's young man, in the army, you know," and that was all that mattered to them, as if he had already made the supreme sacrifice and had earned the respect of every patriotic English citizen.

The path towards the Wrekin took them through a meadow silvered with flowering grasses, brightened with the flare of buttercups and darker patches of rust-coloured sorrel. They walked in single file along a trodden path, Martin striding easily, Serena picking her way more carefully, so that occasionally he had to stop and wait for her. Used to seeing her in formal London clothes, he thought she looked even more attractive in a white pin-tucked blouse which fitted her body closely, and a swinging dark-green skirt, beneath which he caught glimpses of her shapely legs and small feet clad unfamiliarly in thick socks and walking shoes. A straw hat rested lightly on her springy hair, which was tied back loosely so that it hung down her back like a dark waterfall. Dressed like this, she seemed younger than she had appeared at the London parties, and a little shyer of him, so that although she knew the route and he did not, he felt as much in control as if he were leading his platoon on a training exercise.

The path rose gradually, past small farms and through fields of sheep, and now the bulk of the Wrekin rose above them. The path entered woodland, climbing more steeply. Soon, they came out to the summit of a small hill clear of trees, where only the emerald shoots of infant spruce competed with the vivid pink of fox-gloves. The river curved away below, and smoke rose from a chimney in the valley; somewhere a cuckoo called.

"Not far now," Serena panted, "but first we've got to drop down there, and then climb again."

She pointed to a sweep of trees rising to the summit, which now appeared a very long way ahead.

After the short descent, the path rose more steeply than before, so that they had to pause several times for breath. Once or twice Serena lost her footing on the incline made slippery with dried pine needles, and Martin took her hand and pulled her up. Eventually they emerged from the trees on to a smooth plateau, whose grassy surface was broken by a rocky outcrop. Walking more easily now on the comparatively level ground, they made their way along to the summit, marked by a second scattering of rocks. Here, they sat down to rest, and Martin took a bottle of ginger beer and some biscuits out of the rucksack he carried. It was warm enough to sit in rolled shirt-sleeves, with just a faint breeze fanning their hair.

"It's worth it for the view, isn't it?" Serena said.

Martin agreed. Gentle hills rolled away like a green sea to the west; farther away, he could make out the more imposing shapes of the Welsh mountains, faint silhouettes in the haze. To the other side, the river Severn was a shining track, winding through its deep gorge, with a plume of smoke rising from industrial Ironbridge. Then he swivelled round to face the south-east. Somewhere in that direction was the Western Front – this time next week he would be heading there, although it seemed impossible to believe that a war could exist anywhere, now, with larks singing overhead and his face warmed by the sun, and Serena beside him. It was more pleasant to look towards Wales, and think of Ireland beyond, and his aunt and uncle's house there, where he had often stayed. One day, he thought, he'd take Serena to Ireland.

She settled more comfortably, leaning back against him, and said, "I wish you could stay longer. It's horrible to think of you having to go back. I wish you had a nice safe job at the War Office or something like that."

"Don't let's talk about it. Let's enjoy our few days while we have them." He put his arms around her and she folded her arms over them, entwining their fingers. He rested his chin on the top of her head, dislodging the straw hat. Her hair smelled clean, freshly washed, and she wore a faint flowery perfume which he remembered from their London meetings.

"I keep thinking I ought to be a volunteer nurse or drive an ambulance or something," she said. "I always feel a bit guilty when I see the recruitment posters. But Father wouldn't let me, even if I wanted to. To be honest, I don't think I'd be much use as a nurse. It sounds dreadful."

"I'd hate you to be one. It's terribly hard work, especially out in France. And you do your voluntary work at the canteen, don't you? You're doing your bit."

"Do you think so?" Serena said, brightening. She turned her head to look back the way they had come. "Did you know these rocky bits have got names, the first one we passed and this one here? They're called Heaven's Gate and Hell's Gate. But I can never remember which lot is which."

He turned her face towards him so that he could kiss her. "I think this one must be Heaven's Gate."

She laughed delightedly and pretended to protest for a moment but then relaxed, leaning into him and parting her lips beneath his. Then, as he shifted his weight so that he could hold her more closely, cheerful voices were heard, and he and Serena sprang apart. A party of hikers was approaching from the direction of Rushton, middle-aged men in baggy shorts and breeches, carrying maps and binoculars. They called out a greeting and then shrugged off their rucksacks and settled themselves on the rocks, taking bottles and sandwich tins out of their packs.

Serena and Martin exchanged flushed, rueful glances.

"Let's start back," Martin suggested, "we can

find somewhere else to sit further along."

They put the ginger-beer bottle and the biscuits back into the rucksack, and walked back slowly, hand in hand. They had hours ahead of them; there was no need to hurry. When they reached the clearing of foxgloves and spruce, Martin said, "Let's stop here for a while."

Thinking of the hikers and their binoculars, he led Serena well away from the path, to a secluded place screened by shrubs. He spread out his jacket for her to sit on, feeling unaccountably nervous. Serena seemed equally self-conscious, settling herself on the ground without speaking or looking at him; there seemed to be a new tension between them. The air was very still, and bees hummed in the foxgloves. He sat down beside her and took her hand in his and stroked the pale unblemished skin. And then he became aware that she was looking at him intently.

"It's all right," she said, very quietly. "I don't mind."

Her eyes were marvellously blue, and wide, like a child's. She reached out her free hand and stroked the side of his face. He was not sure he had understood.

"It's all right," she said again. "I love you. You don't have to worry about it."

Overwhelmed, he pulled her towards him and held her close, his hands smoothing her back and shoulders. He kissed her hair and neck until he realised that she was making small impatient movements, expecting more. They were both equally inexperienced, not sure at what pace things should proceed. He turned her face to him and kissed her, gently at first; she made no resistance, relaxing her weight into his arms. He felt faintly dizzy, his blood singing in his veins. And then they were clinging to each other with fierce intensity and her breathing was as urgent as his. His hands roved over her body and hers over his, and they were pulling at each other's clothes, hands against bare flesh. He pushed her gently back so that she was lying on the grass and with difficulty pulled up her skirt and petticoat, and she fumbled with her undergarments while he turned away, unfastening his trouser buttons. Whenever he had thought about making love to Serena he had been afraid that his nervousness and inexperience would ruin everything. There was no worry now; it was as if they had set something irresistible in motion. He rolled towards her and she took hold of his shoulders as he lowered his weight on to her, and then he pushed her legs apart with his knee, and he felt her hand creep down to guide him. She cried out once as he entered her and then gasped in rhythm with his instinctive thrusts; he thought he was hurting her, and for a moment it seemed a brutal, almost violent act. Then, with an uncontrollable rush and release of tension, it was over. He lay with his face against her neck, avoiding looking at her, rather disappointed that it was finished so quickly. His whole body felt heavy, drained. Rousing himself, he kissed her neck, and her arms tightened around him.

"Martin?" she whispered. "You do love me, don't you?"

"Of course I do," he murmured. Then he shifted himself off her and turned away so that she could adjust her clothing, and he his.

When they stood up, he darted a look at her, feeling as if she were a stranger. The expression on her face surprised him. It was not tender and suppliant, as it had been earlier. It was more as if she had gone through with something she had resolved to do.

Heaven's Gate? Maybe. They had found opportunities to make love on another two occasions during that leave. It was only later, when Martin was on the train on his way to rejoin his unit, that it occurred to him to worry in case he had made her pregnant. Next time they met, in the autumn, he was prepared. He had a three-day leave in London; Serena lied to her parents about staying with a friend for a Red Cross fundraising event, and they booked themselves into a small hotel, giving their names as Lieutenant and Mrs Sheringham. During those few days they decided to become engaged, and to be married as soon as the war was over.

Hell's Gate had come later.

Three years later, Martin could still remember clearly how Serena had looked after that first time. Now at last he understood that it wasn't simply resignation at his ineptitude. She had decided to make him a gift of herself, because she thought he might be killed.

Eavesdropping

Catherine looked up from the book she was reading when she heard voices approaching across the lawn: her mother and Ingrid Fitzwilliam. She hadn't known that the Fitzwilliams were expected, and not wanting yet another exchange of news and gossip she decided to remain where she was, sitting on a wooden bench behind the rose bushes, out of sight from the lawn.

"I'll get Patsy to bring tea out here, under the cedar tree," Delia was saying.

The two women settled themselves in the cane chairs and then Catherine heard Ingrid say, rather hesitantly, "I hope you don't mind my arriving unannounced, my dear . . ."

"Not at all. It's a pleasure to see you, at any time."

". . . But I felt that I must talk to you about something that's on my mind."

Aware that she was eavesdropping, Catherine changed her mind about staying concealed. She was about to rise to her feet and show herself when Ingrid's next words made her sit back again, attending closely.

"To be perfectly honest, my dear, I'm beginning to wonder whether it wouldn't be wise to sell up the house and move back to England, with things as they are. There seems to be more and more likelihood of civil war. I wondered whether you'd had similar thoughts."

"Sell the house?" Delia repeated. "But you've put so much effort into it. And the garden – Maurice would never leave his garden, surely?"

Ingrid sighed. "That is the problem. But I do wonder whether he isn't being rather blinkered about it. The garden isn't everything. As for the house . . . well, we've no son to inherit it. It's such a pity. We would have loved to think of our grandchildren growing up there."

What would Maura say to that, Catherine wondered, remembering her outburst last time they had met? It was assumed that Maura wouldn't inherit the house because she was female; she would marry, and move away to live with her husband, just as it was assumed that Mullaghcleevaun would go to Andrew. But what if Maura didn't meet someone to marry, or chose not to . . .?

"You really think there's a risk of civil war?" Delia sounded almost amused, rather than concerned, at the idea. "There have always been rumours, as long as I've lived in Ireland, but they never seem to amount to more than the odd skirmish."

"I don't know. You remember . . ." Ingrid lowered her voice, and Catherine had to strain her ears to catch her words "the Delaunays' manservant . . . Corcoran, the one who resigned . . . shot dead by Sinn Feiners . . . body found in a barn . . . accused of being an informer . . ."

There was a pause, and then Catherine heard her mother's voice raised in her hostess manner. "Ah, Patsy. Thank you so much. Just put it here, would you. No, don't worry, I'll pour in a moment."

Catherine caught sight of Patsy McCabe's broad back criss-crossed with apron fastenings as she walked across the lawn towards the kitchen, and then Delia picked up the conversation.

"This was something to do with the execution last week, I take it? The man who shot the RIC sergeant?"

"Yes. Apparently this man Corcoran told the Black and Tans who the man was, and where to pick him up, in Lisgarvan."

"Oh, dear, these things do seem to happen." Teacups chinked against saucers. "Sugar? No? I suppose it is worrying when one thinks about it, but surely we're not likely to be involved. It won't take long for the police to get the upper hand, now that they've got these English reinforcements. As for the idea of selling up and going back to England, to be perfectly honest I'd prefer it, for myself. I sometimes wish I'd insisted on keeping a London flat . . . I do miss the social life, and it would be so nice for Catherine to spend the summer season there when she's a year or two older. But Douglas wouldn't hear of moving away from here, of course. Mullaghcleevaun is his pride and joy, for all the terrible expense of its upkeep."

"And of course it will go to Andrew," Ingrid said. "No, you wouldn't want to part with it. Well, I hope you're right about the rumours. Perhaps it will all blow over."

Catherine sensed that Ingrid had wanted to be reassured, to share Delia's view that the sporadic violence was little more than a small local trouble. Remembering the air of tension in Dublin, and Conor's strength of feeling on the subject of the British, she wasn't so sure. It was difficult to see where the killings would end: each murder provided the motive for the next, in a vicious circle of death and retribution. Maura had foreseen what would happen, Catherine remembered, when they had talked in the churchyard: the suspect for the shooting of the

RIC man had been executed without trial, and inevitably revenge had followed . . . Now there would be another arrest, and so it would go on . . . But civil war? When did tit-for-tat killings become civil war? And was it really likely to become so serious that Anglo-Irish people would evacuate the country? She felt that she could see only the surface ripples of something that went far deeper, with cold dangerous currents . . .

"Ah, here's Mr Sheringham. Is he coming to join us?" Ingrid remarked.

Through the screen of rose leaves Catherine could see Martin walking slowly round the corner of the house. He was dressed in tweed trousers and a shirt open at the neck, with sleeves rolled up.

"Martin, do come and have tea," Delia called to him.

Ingrid Fitzwilliam and Martin greeted each other, and Delia said, "I thought Catherine was somewhere about. Have you seen her?"

"No, not since lunch."

Catherine heard the creaking of cane-work as Martin sat down. Having intended to listen only for a few minutes, she now felt compelled to stay where she was, but with Martin's arrival and the mention of her own name she felt even more like a deliberate eavesdropper.

"It was good of you to take her down to the

coast the other day," Delia continued. "I do hope she isn't taking up too much of your time."

Catherine felt herself blushing hotly. How could her mother talk about her like that, in front of Mrs Fitzwilliam! And after she had specially asked her to make an effort for Martin!

"Not at all," Martin answered, to her relief. "I probably enjoyed the outing more than she did. I enjoy her company."

"Well, it's kind of you to take the trouble," Delia persisted. "Catherine really hasn't got enough to fill her time here."

"It's no trouble," Martin said.

"Maura tends to get quite lonely after she's been at home for a few days," Mrs Fitzwilliam remarked. "They miss their school friends, I expect. It's such a change for them, getting used to quiet family life."

"Why don't you send Maura over on Friday, and she can spend the day with Catherine?" Delia suggested. "That would amuse both of them."

"Oh, how kind of you. Maura would love to come."

"Good. We'll expect her at about eleven, shall we say? Now," Delia said briskly, "when you've finished your tea, Martin, why don't we stroll down and look at the pond? There are some beautiful dragonflies."

Furious, Catherine stood up at last and watched them make their way slowly down to the pond. Her mother had taken Martin's arm and was leaning towards him and laughing at something. It was almost as if – Catherine was outraged – she were *flirting* with him. The realisation was so acute that she forgot her anger and embarrassment at being talked about, and stood staring after them.

She jumped suddenly on feeling a furry touch against her ankles, and looked down to see one of Aunt Madge's tabby cats twining itself around her legs.

"Good afternoon, Catherine," Aunt Madge's voice said, behind her. She was making her way slowly along the paved path, supported by her maid Phyllis, with three other cats trotting behind. "We're taking the cats for their afternoon walk. Enjoying the sunshine? The roses are beautiful, aren't they?"

"Hello, Aunt. Yes . . . they are," Catherine agreed lamely. Aunt Madge was evidently in one of her lucid moods today.

The old lady glanced across the lawn towards the trio walking down to the pond, and then shook her head sadly and said, "Edwin should never have gone out there. I should have stopped him."

Catherine, about to ask "Who's Edwin?"

thought better of it as she caught Phyllis's eye. It was no use asking Aunt Madge. She would have to find out from her mother later.

"Come along, dear." Phyllis tugged at the old lady's arm. "Let's go and look for Minerva. She won't have gone far."

"I was just about to remark to Catherine," Aunt Madge said, resisting, "that all this is bound to lead to trouble."

She looked closely at Catherine with penetrating blue eyes, giving the unnerving impression that she knew exactly what Catherine had been thinking.

Dreams

Martin struggled with the bedclothes over his face. In his dream he felt not the cool smoothness of Irish linen, but the cloying stench of gas and mud. He was sinking, choking . . . and somehow Panton was there, wild dark eyes in a pale face, looking at him, accusing him . . .

His own shout jolted him out of the dream. His voice echoed in his ears and his heart raced. For a moment he thought he would either pass out again, or vomit, or both. The room came slowly into focus and he made out the pale shape of the window, curtains swelling with the breeze, and the tall bulk of the wardrobe. He was perspiring, sick with the stench of mud choking him, filling his mouth and nose, dragging him down.

He slowly got control of his breathing and reached out for the glass of water on his bedside table. And then the door of his room slowly creaked open and someone came in.

For a panic-stricken instant he thought it was

Panton, shaped into reality by the force of the dream. The glass of water in his hand tilted, spilling its contents over the bedspread. He dropped it and reached for his bedside table, frantically groping for the switch of the reading lamp.

The still warmth of the afternoon had given way to an unsettled evening, with a rising wind. By the time Catherine had gone up to her bedroom, a fitful breeze stirred the branches of the trees outside, and the curtains ballooned into the room with each strong gust. She had too much on her mind to be able to sleep. Her mother . . . Conor . . . Martin . . . the shootings . . . Fragments of conversation drifted into her mind and lodged themselves there, regardless of her efforts to banish them and sleep.

And then, above the sighings of the wind, she had heard a sound from the next room, a stifled cry.

She sat up and listened, wondering whether she had imagined it, or whether it had been a fox or one of Aunt Madge's cats outside. But then the wind dropped momentarily and she heard quite clearly, from Martin's room, an intense low mumbling and then a cry, a cry of fear, quickly choked off.

She listened for a few moments longer, hesitating, and then got out of bed and pulled on her dressing-gown. She knocked gently on Martin's door, and when there was no answer she opened the door carefully.

"Martin?" she whispered. "Are you all right? It's me, Catherine."

She heard a quick movement, and the bedside lamp clicked on, throwing a pool of light over the bed. Martin stared at her with complete lack of recognition, as if she were a ghost. Then he sighed and slumped back. An empty glass lay on the bedspread and she saw the spreading stain of spilled water.

"I heard you call out," she said, apologetically. "I thought you were having a nightmare. I'm sorry if I made you jump."

"Oh ..." Martin looked at the overturned glass as if he hadn't noticed it before.

"Here, let me – " She came into the room and fetched a towel from the washstand, and dabbed at the spilled water. Martin picked up the glass and replaced it on the bedside table, lifting it carefully and deliberately as if he were an elderly man, his hand unsteady.

Catherine looked at him doubtfully. "There, it's not all that bad," she said, still dabbing, unconsciously adopting the bracing tones of Matron at school. "Shall I take the bedspread off and drape it across a chair to dry?"

Martin stretched out a hand to feel the candle-wick. "No, it doesn't matter. Thank you." He raised himself to a sitting position and leaned back against the headboard, closing his eyes tightly as if trying to blot out what he had seen in his dream. Then he looked at her again. "I'm sorry if I woke you."

"It's all right. I wasn't asleep."

He swallowed hard. "I should have asked your mother to give me a room away from anyone else."

"Don't worry. I usually sleep heavily," Catherine said. Then, realising what he had implied, she added, "Do you mean you often have nightmares like this, and shout out?"

"I think so. The same one."

"How awful," she said. "I hate having nightmares."

The words were hardly out before she realised how childish he must think her. The occasional nightmare after she had frightened herself with a ghost story – how could that compare with the horrors that must wait for him, night after night?

"Can I get you anything?" she offered. "A drink, or something to make you sleep? Mother's got some pills, I think."

"No. Just stay and talk to me for a bit."

He moved his legs aside. She sat down and he smiled at her, still leaning back.

"You look so normal," he said.

"You don't. You look wild."

His hair was tousled into peaks, and his striped pyjama jacket was undone, showing his bare chest faintly shadowed with dark hair. He looked down and pulled the pyjama jacket straight and fastened the buttons, then raked a hand across his head.

"Is that better? I wasn't expecting a midnight visitor."

She thought he looked beautiful, his face moulded into smooth contours by the lamplight, but could not say so. Instead, she asked, "The dream you keep having – is it what you told me about?"

He looked away, towards the window. "Partly that."

"I'm sorry. I wish there was something I could do to help."

"You do help. Just by being here, by listening. Just by being you."

He stretched out a hand to pull playfully at her hair, which hung loose over her shoulders. Then, instead of letting go, he entwined it around his hand; she was not sure what happened next, whether he had pulled her towards him or she had moved of her own accord, or both, but somehow he was embracing her and her face was against his shoulder. His arms were warm and strong, holding her close. His grip tightened and he buried his face in her hair, and she heard him sigh deeply, his mouth close by her ear. She could feel a pounding heartbeat and was uncertain whether it was his or her own. She didn't know what would happen next, what to do, only that she wanted to stay like this, close to him, comforting him and being comforted . . .

And then he gave her a little shake and murmured into her ear, "Catherine, this is terrible. What am I thinking of?"

She pulled back and looked at him. He smiled, shakily, and said, "I shouldn't have done that. Don't be upset with me."

"I'm not. I liked it," she said honestly.

"Oh, Catherine . . ." He put his hands on her shoulders and kissed her cheek, but then held her away from him, looking into her face. "You're a lovely girl, has anyone told you?" he said in a lighter tone. "It's very nice of you to visit me in the middle of the night. But you must go back to your own room before I do something silly, and get both of us into trouble."

"I'm sorry," she said, embarrassed.

"Don't keep apologising. I should be the one to do that. Now you really must go. How could we explain if your mother came up and found us like this?"

She rose to her feet. "You won't have night-mares again?"

"I don't think so. Not now. You've chased them away." In spite of urging her to go, he let his hand slide down her arm as she stood up, and he took hold of her fingers and squeezed them. "Thank you."

"Goodnight, then."

She almost fled out of the door, closing it with an unintended thud. Back in her own room, she flung herself into bed and pulled the covers up around her ears. She felt as if her skin were tingling from the contact with another warm human body, her nerve ends newly sensitised. She had wanted nothing more than to stay there, held securely in Martin's arms; he had wanted her to stay, too, he had implied. Her thoughts raced, picturing what would have happened if she had. It was like entering into a game with rules and procedures unknown to her. She knew the mechanics of what was supposed to happen, but little else, apart from what she had read in romantic novellas sneaked into the dormitory at school. Martin, she thought, did know; his hands had been strong and confident, he had deliberately held himself back. The thought alarmed and excited her. She thought of the thin wall separating them and wondered whether he would lie awake too, thinking of her.

"Don't go imagining that Martin's in love with you," her mother had warned. But was it really impossible that he could love her? Because he was seven years older? Seven years might seem a lot now, but when they were older – when she was twenty and Martin was twenty-seven – it would hardly matter. There was a bigger age gap between her mother and her father . . . Perhaps, if she were the one person he could talk to, the one person who could understand . . .

And, just as importantly, was she in love with Martin?

The way she felt now, unable to think of anything except his arms around her and the way he had looked at her as if she were a desirable female, no longer a child, there could be little doubt. She had always loved Martin, for as long as she could remember.

A Visit from the RIC

Martin was late coming down to breakfast next morning. Catherine, determined to avoid catching his eye for fear she would give herself away, was disappointed nevertheless when he took little notice of her. He sat next to her father and began discussing the weather, and the likelihood of the crops being harvested within the month, a topic on which she had never before heard him express the slightest interest. He looked refreshed and alert, as if he had enjoyed a good night's sleep. There was no hint that his rest had been troubled by nightmares, nor, Catherine thought ruefully, by sleepless pangs of love. She herself had lain awake until dawn, thinking of nothing but Martin. She ate her toast, wondering whether she had merely dreamed about the night-time encounter. In spite of herself, she kept stealing glances at him while she ate. There was a small nick of blood on his upper lip where he must have cut himself shaving, the only blemish in his otherwise neatly groomed appearance.

"What are everyone's plans for today?" the colonel asked, folding his napkin.

"Martin and I are going to play golf this morning, aren't we, Martin?" Delia said.

Martin nodded, and the colonel said, "Is Catherine going too?"

"Oh, no, Catherine's not a golfer," Delia said smoothly, before Catherine could reply. "And you said you were going to practise the piano, darling, didn't you? You've hardly played at all since you came home. It's too bad of you."

"*You* said I had to practise," Catherine corrected her.

Martin looked at her directly for the first time, and she thought she saw amusement in his glance; whether because of her sharp rejoinder or because she sounded like a petulant child, she was unsure.

"We'll go as soon as you've finished your breakfast, Martin," Delia said. "It looks as if it might rain later."

"If everyone's busy, I may as well get on with the accounts," Colonel Enright said. "Leave the drawing-room door open while you practise, Catherine. I like to hear you play."

"It'll only be scales and arpeggios, nothing very melodious," Catherine said, feeling scratchy. She immediately felt mean. It wasn't her father's fault. Perhaps he disliked the idea of Delia going off with Martin as much as she did. "I'll play something nice for you at the end," she conceded.

"You must play for us one evening," Martin remarked.

Delia rose from the table. "I think she's a little out of practice for public performance, just yet. Maura Fitzwilliam's the one to ask, if you like the piano – she plays beautifully. I'll ring for Kerrigan to bring the car round."

Neither Catherine's mind nor her hands would co-operate with the piano practice. She soon gave up, flexing stiff fingers. Her mother was right; she hadn't practised enough recently. She played her father's favourite Bach prelude, very badly, and then closed the lid of the piano and wandered out into the sunlit entrance hall.

The summer was slipping away, the days passing meaninglessly. She was unsure what to do with herself for the rest of the morning, and felt ashamed of herself for her lack of purpose. She had counted on being able to talk to Martin, and perhaps suggesting a walk or a drive. She hadn't reckoned on her mother commandeering him. Delia was an accomplished golfer and had won tournaments in England in her youth; Catherine imagined her striding about the links, showing off her prowess for Martin's benefit. Had he noticed the coquettishness, Catherine wondered? Was he embarrassed by it, or – she hardly liked to admit the possibility – did he enjoy it? Delia was an attractive woman, undoubtedly; most men would be flattered. Perhaps she thought that flirting with him was the best way to help him over his war trauma, Catherine thought savagely.

She drifted towards the kitchen, her instinctive refuge when she felt worried or depressed. There was something infallibly comforting about the routines of preparing and cooking food, and in Patsy's calm presence. She went in, rather disappointed to find Bridie, the new maid, there with Patsy, pouring cream custard into small ornamental moulds.

Bridie looked up from her task, surprised to see Catherine, and bobbed a curtsey.

"There's no need for that," Patsy told her. "Miss Catherine often comes in for a talk."

Catherine sat down at the scrubbed table. Bridie asked after Martin, and Catherine told her that he seemed much better, not mentioning the nightmares. She watched the girl's deft movements as she cleared away the utensils she had been using. Bridie's hands were small and neat, but reddened and roughened from constant immersion in hot water, unlike the flawless skin of her face. Catherine wondered where she came from and what her home life was like; Bridie lived down in the village, not on the premises like Patsy. Perhaps, at the end of her day's work, she had to go home and look after aged parents, or younger brothers and sisters; it was not uncommon, Catherine knew. For all her interest in the other girl, she felt that Bridie's presence limited the conversation, and was glad when Bridie excused herself to do the dusting upstairs.

Patsy brought a bowl containing carrots and onions from the vegetable rack in the scullery and placed it on the table, and Catherine said, "I'll chop those for you, if you like."

"You'll make your eyes sore and your hands smell of onion," Patsy warned.

"It won't matter. I can wash them afterwards."

"Well, here you are so. Don't be cutting yourself with that sharp knife. Chop them finely now, they're for soup."

Catherine began cutting and slicing, watching the silvery rings of onion slither apart.

"And how is it you're hanging round with time on your hands this morning? Has your mother not arranged anything for you to do?" Patsy asked.

"I'm supposed to be practising the piano. Mother's taken Martin to play golf."

Patsy began peeling potatoes, turning them

rapidly in her hands so that the peel curled from her fingers into a bowl. "You've been spending quite a bit of time with young Mr Sheringham, so I see?"

"A little." Catherine knew she was blushing, and Patsy looked at her shrewdly.

"Ah well, it's no surprise if you're soft on him. He's a handsome young man. And your mother's guessed about it?"

"I don't know. I think so." Catherine was blinking furiously now as the sharp fumes from the onions stung her eyes.

Patsy passed her a napkin. "There, didn't I tell you that'd happen. Do you want me to carry on?"

"No, thank you. I'll finish it." Catherine took the cloth and dabbed at her eyes.

Patsy continued peeling and remarked, "There's no harm in your mother knowing about your cousin, but there'd be trouble if she found out about you seeing Conor."

Catherine looked at her with streaming eyes. Patsy must have seen her coming or going from the cottage; she didn't miss much. Or had Conor mentioned it? He and Patsy were old acquaintances, but surely he wouldn't have made a point of telling her. Picking up the knife, Catherine carried on chopping.

"I've only seen Conor once – twice," she protested.

"And if you left it like that it'd probably be for the best. Conor's very fond of you, you know that."

"And I'm fond of him. It doesn't matter, does it? Am I supposed to ignore him?"

"I'm not criticising you for it," Patsy said. "But I wouldn't want to see you get yourself upset. Conor and your cousin – they've their own problems to see through, the both of them."

With swift movements of the knife Patsy cut the peeled potatoes into neat cubes, which she scooped up and threw into a saucepan.

"I got a lecture from Mother about Martin," Catherine said. "She thinks I'm too young, I'm imagining things, silly things. Perhaps I am."

She couldn't help feeling warmed by the knowledge that Conor was fond of her, but at the same time she felt amazingly fickle, to be entertaining romantic feelings for two people at once.

"There, amn't I giving you another lecture. I didn't mean it to sound like one." Patsy filled the pan with water and set it on the range. "It's hard for Conor. It was bad timing, your father getting him to clear out the cottage, just now."

"Why just now?" Catherine pushed the

chopped onions aside and began on the carrots.

"Coming back, with Major Andrew staying on in the army, and your English cousin staying as well, and you so taken up with him."

"I've never thought of Martin as being English. He's just Martin," Catherine said. "And Mother's English, as well. Andrew and I have both got English grandparents. Martin's no different from us." The chopped carrot fell away from the knife in regular discs, toppling like falling dominoes. "Patsy," she said slowly, "do you think there's going to be a civil war?"

Patsy scooped up the thin slices of onion on a fish slice and flipped them into a frying pan.

"There's always been war, of a kind," she said. "And I can't see it ending until we're allowed to govern our own country."

"Martin played very well," Delia remarked at lunch. "You remember that tricky fifteenth hole," she said to her husband, "the one where you have to cross the stream by the wood? He did a quite magnificent drive, left us all gasping, and did it in three. After he'd been telling us on the way that he was no good at all. The Delaunays have asked us back again to play next week."

"Beginner's luck," Martin said.

"There's no need for false modesty." Delia

looked at him archly across the table. "Even Christopher Delaunay was impressed, and that's no easy achievement, I can tell you."

Catherine pushed her empty dessert bowl away and looked from Martin to her mother and back again. She hadn't realised that the Delaunays had been involved in the golf. She had imagined just the two of them, her mother showing Martin how to get a good swing and follow through, standing behind him to lean over his shoulder with her hands guiding his on the club, the way instructors did. So it hadn't been like that at all.

Glancing up, she caught a glimpse of a black motor vehicle turning the corner of the driveway.

"And how was the piano practice?" her mother asked.

"All right, thank you."

"You didn't practise for very long," the colonel said.

"So what else have you been doing this morning?" Delia asked smoothly.

"I talked to Patsy in the kitchen."

Catherine saw a small frown crease her mother's forehead and knew that she would be reprimanded later, but at that point Patsy came in and said to the colonel, "There's a Sergeant Creel from the RIC here to see you, sir. Coffee's in the drawing room," she added to Delia.

Colonel Enright, looking surprised, pulled himself to his feet and followed Patsy out of the room.

"Oh, dear. Not another incident, I hope," Delia said vaguely. "I suppose we'll hear about it in good time. Shall we go through and have our coffee?"

She pushed her chair back, and Catherine and Martin followed. They made perfunctory conversation while they waited, all of them more interested in the conversation taking place in the study. They did not have to wait long. Delia had barely poured the coffee and handed it round when Colonel Enright came back in, accompanied by two men in the dark bottle-green uniform of the Royal Irish Constabulary. Martin stood up, and the colonel introduced the visitors.

"My wife . . . our daughter, Catherine . . . and, ah, Mr Sheringham, our nephew, who's staying with us. Sergeant Creel and Constable . . . ah . . . forgive me . . ."

"Ewart, sir," the younger policeman supplied.

". . . Yes, Constable Ewart, thought it best to speak to all of us together."

"Won't you sit down and have some coffee?" Delia invited.

"Thank you, Mrs Enright. I will."

"Constable Ewart?"

"No thank you, ma'am."

Catherine watched Sergeant Creel in fascination as he drank; he had a grey moustache with long ends which dipped into his coffee cup. Everyone else waited expectantly. Then the sergeant replaced his cup, wiped his moustache with a handkerchief and said, "I've just been explaining to Colonel Enright that we're calling on a number of houses following a murder believed to have taken place in the vicinity during the last week."

"A murder?" Delia repeated.

"Yes, Mrs Enright. The victim was a man called Corcoran. Until recently he was employed by Mr Christopher Delaunay, who I believe is an acquaintance of yours."

"Mr Delaunay told us about it this morning," Martin said. "Apparently this man Corcoran was believed to be an informer."

The sergeant nodded. "That's right, sir. He'd received threats, so it seems."

"Has the . . . ah . . . body been found?"

"Yes, sir. He was found in a barn on a farm near Lisgarvan. He'd been shot four times, and there was a note in one of his pockets saying the IRA had killed him. Execution, of course, they call it."

"Terrible, terrible," the colonel muttered.

"Do you have any idea who was responsible?" Delia asked.

"We have an idea that the IRA gunmen concerned come from this locality, Mrs Enright. That's why we're visiting houses near by to warn residents to be on their guard. Be careful about keeping firearms under lock and key; keep doors bolted at night. And do report anything out of the ordinary, any strangers in the area."

Delia frowned. "We haven't seen any strangers, have we, Douglas?"

The sergeant replaced his empty coffee cup on the tray and nodded his thanks to Delia, then turned to her husband. "How many staff do you employ here, Colonel Enright?"

Catherine remembered Maura asking her the same question when they had talked in the Fitzwilliams' garden. The colonel's response, like hers then, was to pause while he worked out the answer.

"Not as many as we used to have . . . we've a housekeeper, Mrs McCabe . . . a gardener, or these days more of a chauffeur cum handyman, Paddy Kerrigan . . . a maid, a young girl . . ."

"Mrs Logan, who comes from the village to do the laundry," Delia added.

"Any casual staff?" the sergeant enquired.

The colonel shook his head.

"Just Conor," his wife reminded him. "Paddy Kerrigan's son, who's helping out temporarily."

"And these staff have been with you for a good while?"

"Oh, yes," Delia said, "they've been here for years – apart from the new maid, Bridie. But she comes from the village and we know her father."

"We've always prided ourselves on good relationships with our staff," the colonel said. "And I think their length of service is, ah, testimony to that."

"Thank you, sir." The sergeant rose to his feet. "Well, I think we've taken up enough of your time. It's to be hoped there's no cause for alarm, but do let us know if you see or hear of anything. Good afternoon to you, sir, madam."

Colonel Enright went into the hallway to see the policemen out. Martin and Catherine exchanged concerned glances, while Delia busied herself with clattering the teacups together on the tray, not looking at either of them. Then, when her husband returned to the drawing room, she burst out angrily, "Is that man really suggesting we should be suspicious of our own staff? Are we supposed to imagine that Patsy goes around the countryside at dead of night shooting policemen?"

The colonel sat down heavily and stared at the hearthrug, not appearing to have heard her. "It's a dreadful state of affairs, dreadful," he said, more to himself than to anyone else.

Martin answered Delia's question. "It does sound ludicrous, put like that. But then obviously someone's doing it."

"We've had so little to worry us in these parts, apart from the shooting of that policeman," Delia said. "There's been the odd outburst in Dublin, of course, but apart from that most of the real trouble has been down in Cork and Tipperary."

"What did Mr Delaunay say about the killing?" Catherine asked. "You said he mentioned it this morning."

Her mother stared at her. "Yes, he did, of course. The man left his employment a few weeks ago. Christopher knew nothing about whether he really was an informer or not."

"Perhaps that man deserved it, if he was a spy," Catherine said. "After all, someone else was executed without trial because of what he did."

"Really, Catherine," Delia said in a shocked tone, "where do you get such ideas from? At least the Delaunays aren't getting hysterical about the situation, like some people seem to be. As far as I can see it's just a bunch of hot-heads fighting it out among themselves. I do wonder, Martin, what you must be thinking of this wayward little country? I expect you'll be glad to get back to civilisation."

Not responding to her levity, Martin sat forward in his chair and said in an undertone, "Do you think we're at any particular risk here?"

"Any particular risk? Why should we be?"

"You know . . ."

Delia's face expressed incomprehension. Catherine looked from one to the other, puzzled. Then the colonel lit up a cigar and passed the tin to Martin, who shook his head. "Who's getting hysterical?" he asked, picking up his wife's previous point.

"Oh – Ingrid Fitzwilliam. She was talking of selling up the house and going back to England. It was just talk, as Maurice would never agree to it. Though I must say," Delia said, "the idea does have its attractions."

Colonel Enright looked outraged. "Pack up and run for cover, as soon as there's a little trouble? That would be playing straight into the hands of the Shinners."

"That's what I told her," Delia said.

Picnic in the Hills

"This was a good idea of yours, my dear," Colonel Enright shouted to his wife above the noise of the engine. "It's a while since I've been up in the hills."

It was pointless for anyone to try to answer, since any reply would have had to be shouted two or three times before the colonel heard it. Besides, it seemed unwise to divert his attention from the handling of the car. He was not a confident driver: he had already clipped a gate post by turning a corner too sharply, and alarmed Catherine by swerving perilously close to the hedges each time he turned round to address his back-seat passengers. Usually, he would have asked Paddy Kerrigan to drive, but today there was no room for an extra person in the car. Catherine, sitting in the back between Maura and Martin, would have felt far safer if Martin had been driving. She thought of their outing to the coast, wondering whether the rapport they had established then could ever be regained. If only her mother hadn't invited Maura today ... with Maura present, there would be little chance of any private conversation with Martin.

She could feel the faint pressure of his thigh against hers, and occasionally when the car swung round a bend her weight was tilted against him. But he seemed withdrawn this morning, turned slightly away from Catherine and regarding the scenery moodily. He would be bored soon, she thought, tired of their company and the limited scope of their social life. Then he would go back to England, presumably to take up work in his father's publishing company. The days were slipping away and he would soon be gone. Catherine hated to think about it. His absence would leave a dreadful hollow in her life, a void which could not be filled by any amount of picnics or dinner parties or outings. Her imaginings of two nights ago seemed foolish, the romantic fancy of a naïve schoolgirl. He would go home to England and forget about her.

The car turned uphill, leaving the village behind. There were a few whitewashed cottages on the cultivated slopes of the hillside, with rough hedges straggling some way up before giving way to heather and gorse. Above, the hillside rose smoothly to its summit, beneath a sky of perfect summer blue, silky and streaked with pale cirrus. The car climbed more slowly now. A black and white dog sunbathing in the dusty road dashed to safety just in time, and a peat digger leaned on his spade to watch the car go by, his tanned face impassive. The track rose, winding, until the cottages and farmsteads were completely out of sight, hidden by the swell of gorse-covered hillside. A few sheep scattered as the colonel pulled the car off the track and brought it to rest on a level patch of grass overlooking a wooded valley, and the undulating hills to the south. Everyone got out of the car and removed all the picnic paraphernalia – rugs, hats, cushions, hamper, the colonel's binoculars and shooting stick. It was too early to eat, so the colonel settled himself with his binoculars to look out for birds, while Delia took out a fountain pen and notepad, saying she was going to catch up with some letters.

"Let's walk up to the top of that hill," Maura suggested to Catherine, pointing to a nearby rounded summit. "We'd be able to see down to the city from there."

Martin, after a moment's hesitation, said he would go too, and the threesome began to walk up a meandering sheep's path. It was already so hot that Catherine began to think that a swimming party at the beach might have been more appropriate. The heather was dried and stiff, with peaty soil beneath, but the occasional boulder lay hidden and before long Catherine stumbled against one, almost overbalancing. Martin caught her arm to steady her; righting herself, Catherine noticed Maura's sidelong, amused glance, and knew that Maura thought she had tripped deliberately.

They climbed for a few minutes without speaking, and then Martin said, "I can't help wondering, after what those policemen said last night, whether it's really safe to be walking around like this, miles from anywhere. After all, the Dublin mountains used to be a regular place for Volunteer drilling and exercises."

"What policemen?" Maura was walking hurriedly, keeping a little ahead of the other two.

"Two RIC men came round to warn us to keep doors locked and to report it if we saw any strangers around," Catherine told her.

"I see," Maura said, and then, to Martin, "So you think there might be armed marksmen lurking around the hilltops in the hope of taking potshots at any stray picnickers who might happen to come along? That would be an enormous help in advancing the cause of Irish independence, wouldn't it?"

"It's not as ridiculous a suggestion as you seem

151

to think," Martin said. "You must have read the newspapers. Anyway I was just concerned for you two girls."

"How kind of you." There was a sharp edge to Maura's voice. "I'm sure in that case we've nothing to worry about. If anyone fires at us you can leap in front of the bullets and save us. That would serve two ends at once, I suppose. You'd feel that honour was satisfied, and the bullets would have reached a suitable target."

"Maura!" Catherine reproved.

Maura gave a slight shrug and walked on ahead. Catherine looked at her resentfully, wondering why she was in such a prickly mood; it seemed she was determined to pick an argument. Martin's remark had been harmless enough. Catherine glanced at him, and he gave her a wry look, eyebrows raised. Then he said to Maura, "I'd forgotten you were a Republican."

"I didn't say I was. But it seems to me that the British government has only itself to blame for what's happening. They've banned Sinn Fein, and put the leaders in prison – people who've been fairly elected. What else is there for nationalists to do, other than turn to violence?"

"So you don't think much of the new Home Rule Bill?" Martin said.

"It's completely useless, as far as I can see. It's not going to suit anyone. In fact it's no different from what was offered before the war. Home Rule, not real independence, and a divided country. That wasn't what thousands of Irishmen fought and died for."

"You seem very well informed on the subject," Martin remarked.

"For a girl, you mean?" Maura queried.

"I didn't say that."

"No," Maura conceded, "but I think it's what you meant. Why shouldn't I be well informed? It's my country, and my country's future that's at stake."

Catherine looked from one to the other, fruitlessly trying to think of some remark which would smooth over the unexpected hostility between them. Martin said nothing, but walked on, tight-lipped, looking down at his feet as if suddenly he needed his whole attention for the effort of walking. Catherine looked at him uneasily. They were approaching the summit of the hill, marked by a few boulders piled together to make a small cairn. The level ground dropped away abruptly on the farther side so that suddenly the city of Dublin was spread out before them as if on a map, in bluish haze pierced by chimney-stacks and overhung with flattish palls of smoke. To the east, the Irish Sea was a sheet of metallic blue, its surface undisturbed except by a mail boat which appeared to be as unmoving as a speck on a mirror. Catherine shaded her eyes with a raised hand and tried to pick out identifiable features of the city. After a few moments, she realised that Martin wasn't looking at the view at all, but was sitting on one of the rocks of the cairn with his elbows resting on his knees and his face in his hands.

She went to him at once.

"Martin, what's the matter?"

He looked up at her and she saw the gleam of perspiration on his nose and cheeks.

"I'm sorry," he said. "After all that time keeping my head down in the trenches I can't bear to stand in an exposed spot. I keep looking for enemy snipers. I know it must sound ridiculous."

It was hard to resist the urge to embrace him. "It isn't. It's quite understandable. What shall we do? Do you want to go back?"

He got slowly to his feet. "I'll start to walk back down."

"Let me come with you."

"No, don't. Stay with Maura. I'll be better on my own. I'll see you later on back at the car."

He sounded so definite that Catherine did not persist, and he set off at a quick pace, retracing their steps of a few moments earlier and soon dropping out of view. Catherine watched him unhappily.

"I wouldn't waste your time worrying about him," Maura said. She was still facing the opposite direction, looking out towards the sea, but Catherine realised that she must have overheard the conversation. "That's what he wants, I expect."

Catherine turned on her angrily. "How can you say that? Why are you being so unpleasant?"

"I didn't intend to be unpleasant," Maura said. "I just don't like being patronised."

"Martin wasn't patronising you," Catherine retorted. "You seem determined to take offence at everything he says. You don't understand. You've no idea what he went through in the war, and how it's affected him . . ."

"And you have, I suppose?"

Maura's expression of amused tolerance infuriated Catherine.

"Yes, I do," she said defiantly. "He's told me about it."

"That's what I mean. It seems to me that he's taking full advantage of all the sympathy you and your mother shower on him. I wonder how much longer he'll try to play on it?"

"Play on it? Why are you being so horrible? You saw him that night when you came to dinner . . . that wasn't play-acting, was it? And he has nightmares, I've heard him shouting . . ."

"All right. He had an awful time in the war.

But I'm sure he's enjoying being the focus of attention, being treated as a romantic hero . . ."

She sounded just like Andrew, Catherine thought. Then an explanation occurred to her and she burst out, "You . . . you're *jealous* . . ."

As Maura opened her mouth in protest, Catherine launched into a new attack. "And what about your famous Republican sympathies? Your mother doesn't seem to feel the same, does she? She wants to sell your house and go back to England! So much for your country's future then, if you clear out at the first sign of trouble . . ."

Maura stared at her, and she saw that her taunt had hit home more forcefully than she had intended.

"Sell the house?" Maura repeated. "Go and live in England? Who said so?"

"Your mother. Didn't you know?"

It was abundantly clear that Maura didn't. Catherine almost regretted having mentioned it, but she was still light-headed with anger at Maura's criticisms of Martin and in no mood to capitulate.

"Well, that's something for you to think about, then," she concluded. "And now I'm going after Martin."

She left Maura standing by the cairn, and plunged down the hillside. She was sure that her instinctive accusation had been right; Maura's taunts could only stem from jealousy. Maura had guessed how close she and Martin had become, and was envious. The idea was rather satisfying. For a moment Catherine almost felt sorry for her, and wondered whether to go back; the thought struck her, too, that she should not have repeated something Mrs Fitzwilliam had told Delia in confidence. But she could not forgive the derisive remarks about Martin, and Maura's sarcasms echoing in her mind propelled her down the sheep path with furious energy.

It was very hot now. Her poplin blouse stuck to her skin, and she could feel the trickle of sweat between her shoulder blades; the waistband of her skirt was too tight, uncomfortable. There was hardly a breath of wind, even at this height.

She came across Martin sitting on a rock by a small stream, smoking a cigarette. She had forgotten that he smoked sometimes; it reminded him of her father and Charles smoking together after dinner, and made him seem older, remote. Hearing the brush of her shoes against dried vegetation, he turned and looked at her. His expression showed no pleasure, merely resignation at being interrupted in his thoughts. She was disappointed.

"Where's your friend?" he asked.

"Maura's not my friend. Mother keeps inviting her for some reason. And now I've quarrelled with her."

"What about?"

"About you," Catherine said.

Martin seemed mildly surprised, but did not ask what she meant. Catherine sat down on the cushiony heather beside him and said, "I'm sorry she was beastly to you just now. I don't know what's the matter with her today."

He shrugged, evidently not interested in Maura, and returned to his contemplation of the peaty stream. Lower down the slope, the car was visible; Colonel Enright had wandered a short distance down the wooded valley, and Delia was lying on the rug, apparently dozing.

"I am sorry you felt bad up there," Catherine said. "I hoped . . . I thought things would get better for you, now that you've talked about it. They say it's best to talk about problems, don't they, not bottle them up inside?"

Martin exhaled smoke. "Psychiatrists, you mean? Yes, they have their theories."

A pale spider was clinging to the hem of Catherine's skirt; she watched it with detached interest. "You don't believe in them, then? The theories?"

"I don't really know what I think. Except – look, Catherine, it's hopeless even trying to

158

explain. I shouldn't have told you as much as I did. It isn't fair to burden you with it. I can't expect you to understand. No one who hadn't been there could understand."

"It wasn't your fault, what happened. I think I do understand, how you must have felt . . . I tried to, anyway . . ."

"I know you did, and it was kind of you. But there's something else, something that *was* my fault."

"Can't you tell me about it?"

"No, it's no use. I've got to sort it out for myself. It's wrong to involve anyone else, especially someone like you . . ."

"What do you mean, someone like me?"

He glanced at her. "Someone so young, who knows nothing about war."

She was disappointed again, having expected him to say *someone so sensitive*, or *so understanding*, or *so special*. Before, he had treated her as an equal. Now he seemed like the other adults, putting her in her place, dismissing her concern.

"And about the other night," he continued, looking closely at his shoes. "I'm sorry. It won't happen again, I promise you."

Catherine had been frankly hoping that it would. She looked at his profile, his straight nose and firmly moulded chin, and the lips pressed together in a way she recognised.

"I didn't mind, really I didn't," she assured him. "Oh, Martin, I wish you'd talk to me, like you did before. I want to help, I want to know what upsets you so much. *Please* tell me."

He stubbed out his cigarette on the rock and looked at her sharply. "You haven't the faintest idea, then, or you'd thank God you don't know," he said. "And quite honestly if you had any sense at all you'd leave me alone."

He stood up and walked away down the hillside towards the car.

The remainder of the afternoon passed uncomfortably in the sticky heat. When everyone had finally returned to the car, they ate the picnic lunch, shooing flies and other buzzing insects away from the bottles and plates. Delia seemed blithely unaware of the tensions which had developed among the younger members of the group, and chatted about plans she was making for a long-weekend house party.

"When you go home tonight, I must give you the invitation to your mother and father for dinner on Saturday," she told Maura. "And I hope you'll come too, of course. I'm so pleased that Andrew will be able to join us for the weekend. The Frasers are coming over from London and it's years since they saw him. Did you ever meet Celeste and Simon Fraser, Martin?"

"I don't think so." Martin appeared to be as unexcited as Catherine by the prospect of yet another round of introductions and formal meals.

When the remains of the picnic had been cleared away, Maura got out a book, *Women and Labour*, and sat in the shade of a low tree to read it. The colonel settled down for a nap and Martin went off on his own, down into the wooded valley. Delia decided that she and Catherine should go for a walk together, and Catherine, having quarrelled with Maura and now with Martin as well, had little choice. She spent the next half-hour or so listening to her mother's opinion of Maura – what a nice, intelligent, sensible girl she was, and how she really needn't look such a fright if only she could be persuaded to get herself some decent clothes and visit a fashionable hairdresser.

It was late afternoon by the time they drove through the village on their way home. The main street looked hot and dusty. A few chickens pecked about listlessly and the usual ragged children played a dispirited game in front of the store. Passing beneath the arching trees which made a tunnel of the road as it left the village, the car passed a big black and white horse clopping along in the direction of Mullaghcleevaun; the colonel slowed down to pass it, and Catherine looked up at the rider. Conor. She realised that he must be on his way up to the house to get on with his work at the gardener's cottage.

It wasn't fair, she thought; Conor must already be hot and tired from his day's work, and now he was going to work all evening as well, to earn a few extra shillings for his household.

Tans

Peadar O'Meara rarely slept undisturbed, and on a hot summer's night the bed he shared with his two older brothers was uncomfortably hot and dishevelled. Finding himself squashed against the wall, he gave a practised shove at his nearest brother, Seumas, who grunted and rolled over. Then Peadar realised that it wasn't just the heat and the sweaty closeness of Seumas that had woken him. He could hear the sound of an engine outside, and as he sat up and thumped the crushed pillow into a better shape, the bright light from headlamps swept round, piercing the thin curtains and briefly illuminating the crucifix above the chest of drawers and the small clock which stood there. It was two in the morning, a strange time for anyone to be driving about.

Then he heard voices shouting. Extricating himself from the tangled sheets, he crawled to the foot of the bed and went to the window to look out. The vehicle was a lorry, the sort the army used, and it had just pulled round in the widest part of the town's main street and stopped outside the draper's store. Dark figures emerged from the lorry and then Peadar heard the crash and tinkle of breaking glass.

"Padraig! Seumas! There's men breaking into Noonan's!"

He grabbed each brother firmly by the shoulder and shook, receiving no response other than an unpromising groan from Padraig, who could sleep through anything. He darted back to the window and looked out again. There were other shapes in the street now, and the gleam of torches and lanterns, as neighbours opened windows or came out to see what was going on.

Determined not to miss the excitement, Peadar pulled on a shirt and trousers over his vest and pants, and groped under the bed for shoes. He thrust his feet into them, not bothering with the laces. After a few steps out of the bedroom one of the shoes flapped loosely and he realised that it belonged to one of his brothers, but was in too much of a hurry to go back for his own. He went down the narrow stairs in the darkness, spreading his arms against the walls and probing with an outstretched foot for the edge of each stair. Then, reaching the front door, he drew back the bolts and let himself out.

The street seemed to be full of shadowy figures. Voices were raised in shrill protest from upstairs windows, but the breaking of glass continued. Peadar saw a figure silhouetted by the draper's shop front, arms raised, holding a rifle aloft, and then the handle was jabbed fiercely at the window. Glass shattered and fell, and boots crunched on the shards.

Wasn't anyone going to stop them, call the police?

Then someone ran past him, shouting, "It's the Tans, the murthering swine," and he realised that these *were* the police, or the Black and Tans, which was worse.

He hesitated by the safety of his own front door for a moment, wondering whether to go back indoors and make a more determined effort to rouse his brothers, and his parents. But surely they'd come out anyway in a moment – residents were spilling out into the street, in overcoats or nightclothes, and the bolder ones were screaming abuse at the the uniformed men.

Someone grabbed at Peadar's shirtsleeve. "Who is it they're after?"

It was Michael McColgan, a boy of Peadar's own age. As he spoke Michael hurled a stone towards the army lorry in a futile gesture of defiance; it pinged off the side, insignificant.

"How would I know . . . Where are the Noonans?" Peadar shouted.

"Still inside . . . upstairs . . ." Michael pointed

to the windows above the draper's. Frightened faces looked out, Mrs Noonan and two of her children. Peadar knew that Willie Noonan, the father, held Sinn Fein meetings in his house and sometimes gave out pamphlets, but everyone in Kilcarbery knew that he wasn't a gunman. If the Tans wanted to arrest him, why didn't they simply knock at the door?

A group of the men rammed a crowbar at the shop door until it gave way with a splintering of wood, and then they stormed inside. Someone turned on the electric light inside the shop and Peadar could see men inside pulling bales of cloth off the shelves and overturning the haberdashery boxes which had been stacked neatly behind the counter.

Peadar clung to Michael's arm. "Sure, they're wrecking the whole place!"

"Why are they after Noonan?"

"He's a Shinner, eejit."

"What will they do to him?"

An orderly arrest seemed less and less likely. The two boys drifted nearer in horrified fascination, staying close together. At the back of Peadar's mind was the notion that someone in authority must arrive soon to stop the violence, to restore order and get the raiding Tans under control. But who could stop them? The Black and Tans were supposed to be the enforcers of law and order.

Not all the Tans had gone into the shop. Those outside were faced with an outraged crowd, some of whom were trying to get through the shop doorway to prevent further damage to Noonan's stock. One of the uniformed men at the door wrestled with a young man Peadar couldn't recognise, and then another Tan came to his aid and the assailant was flung aside, doubling up on the ground as a vicious kick made contact with his ribs.

"Get back! Keep away from this door!" one of the Tans shouted.

"Amn't I telling you this is a dacent, law-abiding household . . ."

"I'm warning you . . ."

"You've no right, no right at all . . ."

There was another brief scuffle in the shop doorway and then a volley of rifle shots cracked out like a lashing whip. Everyone was startled into immobility for a moment, and then there was screaming and confusion as some people tried to scuffle out of the way while others surged forward. Michael was knocked over, in danger of being trampled, and for a second Peadar thought he had been shot. He grabbed Michael's arm and hauled him upright. He realised that no one had actually been shot, that the Tans had fired over their heads in an attempt to frighten them into submission. But now the Tans in the doorway were holding their rifles lowered, aiming directly at the crowd.

"Move back," a voice instructed. "Go away to your homes. If anyone comes closer I shall give the order to fire."

It was an English voice, carrying easily above the shouting and the jostling, the voice of someone used to giving orders and seeing them carried out. Faced with the menace of lowered rifle barrels, people began to back away, the jeering voices silenced. A small child began to cry near Peadar; he looked down and saw a face turned up to him, the mouth wide open and almost square in distress. Then he heard his own name shouted across the street. His mother was standing with Seumas in the doorway of their home. He pushed his way through the retreating crowd towards them, forgetting the child. His mother grabbed him by the scruff of his neck as soon as he was within reach, angry at him in her relief that he was safe.

She delivered a stinging blow to his backside. "Didn't I tell you often enough to stay out of trouble? Don't be sneaking away like that again! It's surely not safe in your own home these days, let alone out of it!"

Peadar wriggled free of her grip and muttered to Seumas, "Where's Padraig and Da?"

"Gone up the street to Felihy's in case the Tans are after him as well."

Most of the onlookers had retreated to stand at a distance in resentful groups, still glaring at the intruders. Peadar looked across the street towards Noonan's, expecting to see the proprietor frog-marched out and driven away. Moments later, however, the Tans came out of the shop and piled into the back of the lorry, and the men who had threatened the crowd backed slowly towards the vehicle, rifles still levelled in case of last-minute resistance, until they too were near enough to jump aboard. The smashed door of the draper's was left wide open, pulled half off its hinges. Then the driver revved the engine and the lorry pulled away quickly, leaving the townspeople to express their feelings about the invasion and to inspect the damage.

"What have they done to Noonan, the divils?" Seumas said fiercely. "Come on, Peadar."

He darted across the road, followed by Peadar and their mother. Others had already begun to filter into the shop, pausing to look by torchlight at the desecration of Noonan's shop window and stock.

"Put that light on, Jack," someone said.

"I can't. The fitting's been smashed."

"Give me that torch, so. The Noonans are still upstairs, or out the back."

"They'll be terrified out of their wits, poor souls."

"A lot of work it'll take to get this lot straight again."

Someone who had a torch directed its beam towards the window display. The wax dummy which had stood there lay stiffly on the floor, a painted smile fixed incongruously on her lips. The blouse she had been modelling was ripped and torn half-off, so that a pink swell of nipple-less breast lay exposed to the gazers. One of the men fetched a length of curtain fabric and draped it decorously over her, as if she were a real corpse. The torch beams swept on, revealing lengths of Irish tweed, of spotted organdie and cotton ticking and tulle all unrolled and trampled, some of the bales stabbed through as if they were enemies in a bayonet charge. Boxes of cotton reels and buttons and hooks and eyes and rolls of elastic lay toppled over the counter and floor, their contents tipped together in confusion. Even the cash register had been pulled off the desk and had crashed to the ground, its drawer open and coins spilling out. Everyone stepped carefully over the debris, as if their feet could possibly inflict further damage. Shocked and silent at first, they began to give vent to their sense of outrage.

"How can dacent people make a living with those murthering swine roaming the country . . ."

"Sweepings of English prisons, so they are . . . shouldn't be allowed to set foot in Ireland . . ."

"Should be rounded up and shot, the lot of them."

"Shooting's too good for them, so it is . . ."

At that point a penetrating wail made all eyes turn to the back of the shop. Seumas grabbed Peadar's arm and pulled him through the narrow doorway to a corridor which led to the family's private rooms; they paused at the bottom of the stairs but then traced the source of the wailing to a small sitting-room on the ground floor. It seemed to be Mrs Noonan who had cried out; she was sobbing uncontrollably, supported by one of the men who had argued with the Tans at the door. He held the side of her head firmly against his chest as if to prevent her from looking at something on the floor, at which everyone else was staring. One of the men was crossing himself and muttering a prayer; all the adults in the room seemed too shocked to notice Seumas and Peadar as they entered the room.

Sprawled on the floor, half-propped against

the sofa as stiffly as the shop dummy, was Willie Noonan. His eyes stared at the ceiling and blood trickled from the corner of his mouth, which was contorted in a grimace showing all his teeth, like a snared fox Peadar had once seen. Peadar's eyes dropped horrified to the dead man's stomach and abdomen, which were gashed with darkening scarlet. The pattern of the linoleum beneath him was obscured by a stain of dark shining red, and there was blood on Noonan's hands as if he had tried to staunch the flow . . .

And then Peadar started to scream.

Conor

Catherine put her knife and fork neatly together. "That was delicious, Patsy."

Patsy looked sceptically at the cleared plate. "You've a hearty appetite for someone who's supposed to be unwell, I'm thinking. You'll be going early to bed, I take it?"

"Well ... perhaps not just yet. It's a fine evening."

"Don't be forgetting I'm in charge of you the night," Patsy warned. "Tucked up in bed with a hot water bottle and a mug of cocoa, that's where your mother expects you to be."

"It was just a headache, not double pneumonia. And you know Mother won't give me another thought now she's gone."

"You might just as well have gone with them." Patsy took Catherine's greasy plate and plunged it into the sink. "I thought you'd have been pleased to spend an evening at the theatre with your cousin."

Catherine stood up and stretched her arms

above her head. "Perhaps," she said guardedly. "But not just at the moment."

She did not want to think about Martin, who seemed to have been avoiding her since yesterday. It was nice for once to have a free evening, with the house entirely to herself. There seemed to be almost a holiday air about the place tonight, she thought; Patsy was probably looking forward to a few hours of leisure, free from ringing bells and meal timetables. As there was no dinner to cook, Bridie had gone home early, and when Patsy had finished washing the plates and cutlery she picked up a book from the mantelpiece and settled herself in a chair by the range.

"Knock on the door to tell me when you're going to bed, won't you," she told Catherine, "and I'll bring you some hot cocoa. I want to know you're safe in your room."

Catherine left the kitchen and wandered out of the front door into the warmth of the evening. She had no intention of going to bed yet. Conor's piebald horse had been tethered by the gardener's cottage for the last hour, and she wanted to see what Conor was doing. Passing the kitchen window a few moments later, she glanced cautiously in and saw that Patsy was already leaning back in her chair, her eyes closed and the book unopened on her lap.

The piebald horse was munching steadily at

the edge of the shrubbery, grasping shoots of foliage in its mobile lips. Its coarse tail swished rhythmically at flies and it turned its head to look at Catherine as she came near, its jaws continuing to rotate. It was a stocky animal, with large hooves almost concealed by the hair fanning over them. Catherine gave it a wide berth and made her way to the back of the cottage.

Conor didn't hear her approaching. He was whitewashing the walls, his back to her, bending to dip into a bucket on the ground. She went up beside him as he straightened, and touched his shoulder.

"I didn't know you had a horse of your own," she remarked.

He spun round at her touch and looked at her with startled eyes. Then he relaxed visibly. "*Catherine*. Mother of God, I thought . . . You shouldn't creep up on me like that."

"Why? Who were you expecting?"

"No one comes round here, that's why I jumped. The horse, he isn't mine, he belongs to Jimmy Doyle at the forge. I borrow him sometimes. It makes a change to ride up here through the woods."

Then he gave her a more detailed scrutiny, noticing her daytime skirt and blouse, and her hair loose around her shoulders.

"How is it you're out here at this time of

evening? Shouldn't you be having your dinner?"

"I've had tea instead. The others have all gone out. They've gone to Dublin, to the theatre."

He bent down for a fresh brushful of white-wash and slapped it on the wall with long firm strokes. "I saw you in the car yesterday," he said. "Your parents ought to be more careful about driving around the roads in an open car."

"Do you think it isn't safe?"

"You never know who's around. You must know the sort of thing that happens."

"But not to ordinary people, surely? Only to spies and informers, or RIC men. Mother and Father don't think it's particularly risky, not for us. They don't think there's any point in getting hysterical about it."

Slap, slap went the paintbrush, and all the grimy marks and chipped patches and stains on the wall disappeared beneath smooth whiteness.

"What your parents mean," Conor said, "is they don't want to admit there's any risk. If they admitted that, it'd mean they know things are changing. The way of life they lead is changing, coming to an end. And they don't want to think about that, so it's easier to carry on as they always have, and pretend nothing much is happening. That's your father's attitude, at any rate. I wouldn't know about your mother."

He spoke matter of factly, as if stating the obvious.

"It sounds as if you've a grudge against my father," Catherine said.

Immediately she felt foolish. Why shouldn't Conor dislike someone who must represent everything he detested? It was only surprising that he didn't have a similar grudge against her, too.

But he looked at her and said, "I haven't. Your father's been good to me. I've nothing against him. Nothing personal, at any rate."

He paused to rescue a struggling bee which had fallen into the whitewash, lifting it on his forefinger and placing it carefully on a nearby spray of elder. As he bent down Catherine noticed fine white particles clinging to his hair and eyelashes, and in the creases around his eyes.

"It looks fun, whitewashing," she remarked. "I wouldn't mind helping."

"You can, if you like," Conor said. "I've some overalls inside for when I start painting the doors and windows. I didn't bother putting them on for this – it washes off, it's not like proper paint. You could wear those."

Liking the idea, Catherine followed him into the cottage, where everything was now stacked tidily, and he produced the navy-blue overalls from a canvas bag. Holding them against her, he said, "You'd need to roll the arms and legs up."

"I can't get them on over my skirt," she said, realising.

"You'd have to take that off first. It's all right, I'll go outside while you change."

A few moments later she emerged, giggling as she looked down at her legs unfamiliarly clad in heavy cotton, with the trouser bottoms bulkily turned up. "I feel like one of those women who used to deliver coal in London during the war," she said.

Conor grinned. "I've seen the pictures. All you need is one of those turban things, for your hair. Wait, let me tie it back for you. It'll fall down and dip in the bucket otherwise."

He pulled a length of string from his pocket and cut off a piece with his knife. Obediently, she turned round and he gathered up her hair and held it at the back of her neck. His hands were gentle, tickling the sensitive skin. Remembering that he had said her hair was beautiful, she felt suddenly self-conscious.

"There," Conor said, pulling the string tight and knotting it. "That'll keep it out of the way. It'd be better in a long plait really, but I don't suppose you were thinking you'd be decorator's mate when you came out this evening."

"Whatever would Mother say if she could see me like this?"

Conor grinned again. "Wouldn't she blister the ears off both of us."

He handed her a clean brush and she got to work, enjoying the sense of conspiracy. The thought of her mother's outraged indignation if she could see her added a positive pleasure, the spice of doing something forbidden. Besides, the work itself was satisfying; the whitewash went on as smoothly and cleanly as icing on a cake. Soon, between them, they had covered a large expanse in shining whiteness, and Conor fetched a ladder so that he could reach up to the eaves. Catherine steadied the ladder for him and stood below his firmly planted feet, looking up at the worn tread of his boot soles, and passing up the bucket for him to dip into. Every so often he would climb down to the ground and they would move the ladder along a bit further. She watched him, thinking how sure and confident his movements were. It pleased her to be doing something useful and practical, a job that needed to be done.

"There, that's soon finished, with two of us," Conor said at last, clumping down the ladder. "I shan't start another wall tonight. There won't be enough daylight left."

Catherine stepped round the corner to look regretfully at the untouched side wall. "I wish I could come and help you again," she said, "but there won't be much chance of slipping away. We've got guests coming tomorrow and a big dinner on Saturday."

"Who's coming so?" Conor took the brush from her and put it with his in the bucket.

"Oh, Mother's invited some people from London, and Andrew's coming for Saturday night, and the Fitzwilliamses, as usual. As if we haven't seen enough of them. Are you going home now?"

"When I've tidied away here. Go and put your own clothes back on while I wash these brushes."

The light was fading, and there was a coolness in the air. When Catherine was ready, Conor put the bucket and brushes and the ladder away inside the cottage, and they walked round to the front where the horse waited patiently, dozing now with his lower lip hanging and a hind hoof tilted.

"Sure he thinks he's here for the night," Conor said affectionately, putting an arm round the horse's neck. He seemed in no hurry to go, now that he was ready. The piebald turned its whiskered nose to blow at his face, as if he were another horse.

"I wish we had a horse of our own here," Catherine said. "I haven't ridden for years. I used to love it when I was little. And do you remember how we used to look for mushrooms in the horses' field?"

"You can have a ride on old Shamie, if you like," Conor said.

"What, now? Don't you want to get home?"

"I'm not in any great hurry."

Catherine realised that he was as reluctant to part as she was, after the companionship of the whitewashing. It was getting late, and Patsy would be wondering where she was, if she had woken up, but it seemed to be an evening for acting on impulse.

"There's only one horse," she pointed out.

"Shamie can take both of us round the woods." Conor leaned against the horse's pied shoulder, one hand entwined in the long mane.

"Both of us at once? Won't he mind?"

"Sure, couldn't he carry twenty stone and not notice it. You're as light as a feather and I'm no great weight."

"But he hasn't got a saddle," Catherine said, eyeing the horse doubtfully.

"All the better, for two," Conor said.

He untied the tethering rope and knotted it around the horse's neck; then he took a handful of mane and vaulted easily up to its broad back.

Catherine watched admiringly, wishing she had kept the overalls on. She couldn't see how she was going to mount, with no saddle and no mounting block.

"How am I going to get up?"

"Here, give me your hand," Conor said, "and then reach up and put your foot on my foot. No, eejit, the other one. I thought you could ride?"

"Not like this . . ." Catherine said, doing as he told her. And then with one swift movement he pulled her up in front of him so that she was sitting astride Shamie's broad back. She wriggled and hitched her skirt up more comfortably. It felt odd to be riding astride, her legs against the horse's sides instead of the padded bulk of a saddle. Used to the pommels of a side-saddle holding her firmly in position, she would have felt precarious without Conor's arms round her, steadying her and holding the reins.

"I've never been on such a big horse before," she said nervously.

"Ah, he's as quiet as a kitten, old Shamie." Conor clicked his tongue and Shamie moved forward.

For a moment Catherine thought Conor was going to ride in full view of the house towards the gate by the lime trees, but then she imagined hoof marks spoiling the perfection of her father's beautiful lawn and realised that of course he wouldn't. There must be another way into the woods. Sure enough, Conor steered the horse down a track alongside the overgrown vegetable plots. When they reached a narrow gate, she expected him to dismount to open it, but instead he positioned the horse deftly so that he could reach down to the rope fastening. Shamie obliged by pushing the gate open with his chest.

"Mind your legs on the gatepost," Conor warned, and then Shamie pivoted round to face the gate and pushed it to again, and Conor dropped the loop into place. Catherine, surprised that a large and apparently clumsy animal could move with such precision, was impressed. She looked down at Conor's hands which held the reins lightly: suntanned, calloused hands, with fingernails dirt-encrusted and broken, and a long scratch scoring one wrist. A workman's hands, and yet their touch had been gentle on her hair, and when he had rescued the drowning bee.

"Don't sit so stiffly. Let yourself relax," Conor's voice said, close by her ear. "Isn't it as easy as sitting in an armchair?"

Shamie's hooves clopped steadily along the woodland path. A bird gave a startled cry above and flew off with a beating of wings; far off an owl hooted. It was cool in the woods, the smell of foliage mingling with the aromatic scent of pines. It was an enclosed, magical world; Catherine's imagination took hold, and she began to picture herself as the heroine of some medieval romance, being carried away from imprisonment or enchantment by a gallant rescuer ... Shamie, it had to be admitted, was rather on the plain side to be cast in such a role; he ought to be dappled-grey or coal-black, with an arched neck and rolling eyes, and nimbly treading hooves rather than great soup plates ...

Conor reached out an arm to push a dangling screen of silver birch away from Catherine's face. The narrow path they had been following reached a cross-section, and the direction they now took widened into a broad grassy track, bordered by pines.

"Do you want to try a canter?" Conor suggested.

"I'll fall off!"

"You will not. I won't let you."

"Well, if you're sure ..." Catherine said doubtfully.

Conor's left hand in front of her shortened its hold on the reins, and Shamie's head went up, ears pricked. For a few moments Catherine felt herself bouncing as the horse sprang forward into a trot. Conor tightened his right arm around her waist, and then the uncomfortable trotting pace surged into an easy rocking motion.

Uncertain of her balance at first, Catherine found that she could sit into it, swaying with the rhythmic strides. It was exhilarating, the cool air rushing into her face, the twilit shapes of trees looming and then left behind, the horse's forelegs reaching out beneath her. Conor rode easily, his body supple, and his arm held her firmly against him so that she felt herself swaying to the same fluid movement, as if they were both part of the horse. There was no sense of the clash of wills Catherine remembered from her early lessons on a contrary-minded pony; it seemed that Shamie almost anticipated Conor's wishes, and carried them out with surprising agility . . .

And then, all too soon, the ride closed in, Shamie's hooves struck roots snaking across the path, and the riders had to duck to avoid low branches. Conor slowed the pace and let Shamie walk on a long rein. She could feel the warmth of the horse's sides through her stockings. Although she no longer needed Conor's support, his arms were still round her, one hand holding the reins loosely.

"Did you like it?"

"I *loved* it . . . Oh, if only it wasn't getting dark . . . we could have gone on . . ."

Conor brought Shamie to a halt.

"I'll drop you off here and you can walk straight across the garden," he said, and she realised that they were almost at the gate by the lime trees. She did not want to dismount, to leave Conor and bring the wonderful, unexpected evening to an end. But she obediently swung her right leg over Shamie's neck and slithered to the ground. It seemed a very long way down, and she landed awkwardly, pitching forward. Conor vaulted to the ground beside her and dropped the reins on Shamie's neck.

"I was going to get off first and hand you down, like a gentleman."

He was laughing at her as she staggered on wobbly legs, and then he took her arm to steady her, and she clung to him unashamedly, suddenly not knowing whether to laugh too, or cry, because the evening was coming to an end and she could see no prospect of there ever being another like it.

Conor bent down and kissed her on the lips, very gently.

After a moment they drew apart and regarded each other as if shocked by the unexpected turn of events, and then he held her close and kissed her again, with brief, hesitant kisses. Her arms went round him and she could feel the warm litheness of his body beneath his shirt. He smelled faintly of Shamie. It felt natural, inevitable, as if Conor had always been there in the background of her life, waiting for her.

Conor stroked her hair, entwining a hand in the length of it, just as he had grasped Shamie's mane earlier. He pulled her head back a little and looked into her face, and she saw regret and tenderness combined in his expression.

"You'll have to go in," he said. "It's getting dark."

"I don't want to."

He stroked her cheek and said, "Come on. You'll be getting into trouble." He left Shamie browsing in the foliage and went with her to the gate and opened it for her.

"Oh, Conor . . ." She did not know what to say. They were still holding hands, their fingers intertwined.

He lifted both their hands, and kissed her fingers. Then he gave her a little push. "Go on."

She stumbled across the grass towards the lit windows of the house, looking back once in case Conor was still watching her, but it was too dark to see.

Friends of the Family

Very late that night, unable to sleep, Catherine heard Martin go into his room, moving about as he got ready for bed. She turned over resolutely and muffled her ears with the pillow. She did not want to think about Martin. He could have as many nightmares as he liked, and still she would not bother him with her unwanted sympathy.

Nevertheless, for all her determination to banish him from her mind, Martin was unavoidably there, mixed up with her thoughts about Conor. It struck her once again that she must be extraordinarily disloyal, to be attracted to both of them at once. It was the sort of thing disapproved of as *fast*, and what could be more fast than allowing herself to be embraced by two young men within a week?

The ride in the woods seemed like a delicious secret, but it had not taken long for doubt to set in. Had Conor's kiss merely been a pleasant way to end the evening, or did it mean that he cared for her? And even if he did, and she for him, what hope was there of continuing to snatch even brief meetings? If her mother found out, she would dismiss Conor from the premises without compunction. And soon, when he had finished decorating the cottage, Catherine couldn't see how she would be able to meet him at all.

It was hopeless. Conor was a Catholic, and nationalist, and working class. If he had lived on the moon he could hardly have been further out of her social sphere. She imagined saying to her mother, "I'd like to invite Conor to the dinner party on Saturday . . ." ". . . Why don't we ask if Conor would like to come with us to the theatre?" . . . No, it was impossible.

Knowing this made her think of him all the more fondly, with the ache of wanting what she could not have. But something else worried her: the thought that perhaps, without realising it, she had sought out Conor to make up for Martin's rejection, to prove to herself that someone other than Martin found her interesting and attractive. Ashamed of the thought, she pushed it aside, telling herself that her new feelings for Conor were not misplaced. She felt safe with Conor, in a way she hadn't felt safe with Martin. She could trust Conor.

But it was still hopeless.

*

The new dresses arrived from Dublin.

"Just as well," her mother said. "I was hoping the new evening frock would be here in time for Saturday. I don't know what you could have worn otherwise."

Delia was full of enthusiasm for her weekend house party. She threw herself vigorously into the preparations, consulting menus, making plans for drives and golf and beach picnics. Another maid, Mary, had been hired from the village, to get the extra guest rooms ready and to help with the food preparations. Catherine, in spite of herself, was caught up in the excitement of it. Persuaded by her mother, she went upstairs and put on her new dresses one after the other, and paraded them before her parents and Patsy.

"Oh, yes!" her mother approved, as she twirled before them in pale lilac crêpe de Chine with a dropped waist and flared skirt. "That does look stylish. I almost wish I'd ordered one like it for myself."

"You'll turn heads wearing that," Patsy said, "sure you will."

Only Martin seemed unmoved by the prospect of the weekend, unimpressed by the new clothes. Silent and moody, he kept out of the way as best he could, reading the newspaper or going out for walks by himself. In spite of her determination to remain aloof, Catherine noticed his comings and goings, and hoped he would not bump into Conor in the woods.

The Frasers arrived on Friday, collected from the station by Paddy Kerrigan. They were not as old as Catherine had expected – she estimated their age at around thirty – and were very smart, with vast quantities of luggage in pigskin cases, as if they were moving in permanently rather than staying for a long weekend. The husband, Simon, seemed affable enough, rather overshadowed by the more vibrant personality of his wife. Delia had told Catherine that Mrs Fraser had worked as a nurse during the war, and Catherine had been expecting a starchy matron, but Celeste looked like someone who had stepped from the pages of a London fashion magazine. She was not beautiful, but with her striking appearance – unlike anyone ever seen before at Mullagh-cleevaun – and her obvious expectation of being the centre of attention, it was easy to think that she was. She was tall, with dark hair cut very short, curling in close at the nape of her neck, beneath a felt hat with a swooping brim. She wore a short striped coat with an enormous collar, and a narrow calf-length skirt which clung to her legs. Even Delia looked provincial and unexceptional beside her as they clasped each other fondly in the porch like long-separated sisters.

"How *wonderful* to see you . . . such a long journey . . . no, hardly rough at all . . . simply *ages* since we saw you . . ."

Amidst the effusion of greetings Catherine caught sight of her father looking rather bemused, casting startled glances at Celeste. He disapproved of modern women.

Delia introduced him, and then Catherine, and as Celeste turned to grasp her hand warmly Catherine noticed that she was wearing bright lipstick and face powder. In the *daytime*. No wonder her father looked wary. She looked around for Martin, wondering what he would make of the newcomer, but he was nowhere to be seen.

At dinner, expecting to feel awkward and tongue-tied in the company of the elegant visitors, Catherine found that she need not have worried; the conversation was dominated by her mother and the Frasers, so that no one else felt obliged to contribute. The conversation largely revolved around London acquaintances and the theatre, so there was little Catherine could have said even if she had wished to. Celeste told a great many anecdotes about London social life and celebrities, interspersing her remarks with gales of unrestrained laughter, in which her husband and Delia joined.

"My dear, you simply must come over and

stay for a fortnight or so." Celeste leaned towards Delia with a wine glass balanced elegantly between her fingers. "You're getting quite out of touch over here."

Catherine caught sight of her mother's fleeting expression of wistfulness, as if the animated talk had stirred up feelings of regret for the London life she had left. Catherine felt rather disturbed by the glimpse, wondering whether her mother wouldn't prefer to leave the uneventfulness of Mullaghcleevaun behind and go back to London with her guests, to a life of youthful modernity.

Martin said little during dinner, except when directly asked a question. Catherine, sitting next to him, occasionally cast sidelong glances, noticing that he was drinking a good deal of wine, and gradually subsiding into introspective silence. Perversely, it was when he was at his least communicative that she felt most intrigued by him.

When the meal was over, Celeste took a long-handled cigarette holder from her evening bag and inserted a cheroot into its tip. "You don't mind if I smoke, do you?" she asked casually.

Delia waved a hand in permission, and Celeste took out a small silver lighter and lit up, expertly sucking in her breath. The colonel's eyes widened, appalled. As Catherine bent her head to hide her amusement she saw that Martin had noticed, too, and they exchanged brief conspiratorial smiles.

By the following afternoon, the house was a flurry of activity. Delia had taken the Frasers out to play golf, and had managed to persuade or bully Martin into making up a foursome; the colonel, seizing the chance for solitude, had gone for a walk in the woods. Before going out, Delia had given Patsy a long list of instructions, and Catherine found it difficult not to get in the way as Patsy and the two girls worked their way through their tasks with bustling efficiency. They were enjoying it, she thought, surprised that they relished the extra cooking and cleaning and the prospect of a very late night. It was almost as if they were to be guests themselves; indeed, Catherine thought ironically, remembering Martin's gloomy face, they were probably looking forward to it more than some of the guests, for whom dinner-parties were a routine occurrence. She decided to fill in the time by practising the piano, but no sooner had she begun to play, rather diffidently, than Paddy Kerrigan came in to move the drawing-room furniture and rugs aside for dancing later. She went into the kitchen to see if she could help Patsy, and was given some trifles to decorate with candied fruit, but felt in the way there too; Patsy had her own ways of doing things, and it was easier for her to dart around giving sharp orders to the girls and apparently doing six things at once without having to stop for explanations. The food preparations seemed to be well ahead. Catherine had already seen Bridie carrying glazed fruit flans and moulded jellies into the scullery, and the other girl, Mary, had almost finished preparing an enormous mound of vegetables. The two girls had been talking cheerfully as they worked, but fell respectfully silent while she was present. Realising that they would prefer to be left alone to chat about the forthcoming evening and the guests, she left them to their chores and went up to her room.

The new crêpe de Chine dress was hanging against the mirrored door of her wardrobe, ready for the evening. She decided to wash her hair, and sat looking out of the sunlit window brushing it while it dried. It always took an age to dry properly. She wondered what it would be like to have short boy's hair, like Celeste, and then swiftly rejected the idea because Conor had admired her hair as it was.

Andrew arrived home late in the afternoon, dumping his bags in the hall with a proprietorial air.

"I had to get a cab from the station," he complained to Catherine, "and the first driver I asked refused to bring me here. Just sitting there in an empty cab, with no other passenger in sight! Damned insolence."

"It was your uniform, I expect," Catherine said, and then, to placate him, "Would you like some tea? I'll ask Patsy for some. The others will be back soon, and Father's in his study."

"Martin still staying here?" Andrew asked.

"Yes, he is."

"Has he made up his mind yet about working for a living?"

"I don't know. I haven't discussed it with him. Why don't you go and say hello to Father? I'll send the tea in."

"All right," Andrew said, but he stopped to frown at the wooden panelling.

"What are you looking at?" she asked.

"Oh, nothing. This could do with a coat of varnish, that's all. Father really oughtn't to let things go."

Catherine went to ask Patsy for the tea, already needled after less than five minutes in Andrew's company. She knew that the house would be his one day, but she didn't like him behaving as if it were his property already.

"Oh, well done!" Celeste applauded enthusiastically as Martin putted his ball into the final hole. He had played reasonably well, but not well enough; Delia had won, of course, narrowly beating Simon, and now they all waited while Celeste hit several wildly aimed shots from the edge of the green. Martin leaned on his putter to watch. All Celeste's movements were extravagant, rather actressy, he thought, as if she were posing for a glossy photograph. At last she holed the ball and turned to the others in triumph.

"There! An honourable fourth place, even if my score is nearly twice Delia's. Not bad, considering I haven't played for years. I enjoyed that, Delia. I see you haven't lost your touch."

They walked back slowly towards the pavilion, followed by the boy who was caddying for them. It was a very still afternoon, the sun melting into a hazy sky. The chestnut trees which bordered the links were beginning to look autumnal, with small green conkers already visible among the crisping fingers of leaves. Another party of golfers was teeing off for a late game, one of them giving a shout of disgust as his first drive soared off-course.

In spite of the mediocrity of his golf, Martin knew that he had performed better than anyone realised. Before, with Delia and the Delaunays, it had been difficult to quell an irrational fear that the line of conifers bordering the first fairway concealed a ditchful of enemy snipers, and he had eyed each bunker they approached as if it were a shell-hole offering possible cover if a grenade came over. Today, he had been able to laugh at himself, keeping his fears under control, his mind on his strokes and on Celeste's ridiculous antics. He was improving.

"Are there any good golf clubs in Hampstead, Mr Sheringham?" Celeste asked him. She pronounced it *gofe*.

"I believe so. I don't play much."

"You played very well, in that case. You should keep it up. I'm sure your fiancée would enjoy it. Gofe's one of the few games men and women can play together."

He glanced up sharply, noticing Delia's dismayed look.

"I don't have a fiancée," he said.

"Oh, but surely . . ." Celeste's dark brows drew together in a frown. "We know Mr and Mrs Hastings in Highgate. I thought you were engaged to marry their daughter Serena. I'm sure Cynthia said Martin Sheringham."

"Yes. We were engaged, but not any more," Martin said stiffly.

Celeste's face affected concern. "Oh, I'm so sorry. Do forgive me. Have I made a frightful gaffe? But a broken engagement is so distressing. I can see you're upset about it. Is there any chance of a reconciliation?" she asked with characteristic bluntness.

"No," Martin said shortly. "Actually it was my decision to break it off."

"I see." Celeste raised her eyebrows and looked at him with what he took to be disapproval. For all her modern ways, she evidently thought it not quite the done thing for a young man to leave a girl in the lurch.

Delia touched his arm. "Do give the boy a tip, Martin, and let's get on our way home. We'll be in time for a late tea." He knew she was embarrassed by Celeste's remarks. She would regard it as her duty as hostess to forestall any unfortunate turns in the conversation. But then she probably had no more idea than he did that her guests knew Serena's family.

Martin found some coins in his pocket for the caddy's tip, stowed the clubs in the back of the car, and got into the driver's seat. He was pleased that Delia had asked him to drive. He enjoyed being in control, and besides it freed him from the duty of making conversation. He felt more shaken than he cared to admit by what seemed to be a stroke of incredible bad luck. He had come away from London to get away from all that – the overlapping social circles, the friends of friends, the indefatigable interest in other people's problems and relationships . . . the only consolation was that the Frasers evidently did not know Serena's family very well, or they'd have heard about the broken engagement.

He changed gear at the junction and let out the throttle so ferociously that gravel spat out under the wheels. An elderly farm worker on a bicycle wobbled, recovering in time to dart an angry look at the car and its occupants. Celeste giggled, thinking Martin had done it to be amusing, and Delia clutched at her hat and gave him an anxious look. He knew that he would have to be careful or he would sink into another of his black moods, a state of mind in which everything seemed pointless; he felt disgusted and impatient with himself, and yet any activity which might offer an escape from it seemed unbearably tedious, a waste of effort. People were always expecting him to make plans for his future, a career, subjects for which he could summon no enthusiasm . . . when the black mood overcame him, he felt that it was as much as he could do to get through a single day at a time.

He would have to try harder, he knew, with another damned dinner party to get through; he couldn't sit there again like a spectre at the feast, as he had last night. He owed it to Delia, after all the efforts she'd made on his behalf. And to Catherine . . .

He felt bad about Catherine. He thought about her while he nodded vaguely at some remark Simon was making about the suspension in the Vauxhall, and how it compared to his own de Dion. He knew that he hadn't been very nice to her in the last few days; he'd have to try to make it up to her before he left, which he supposed would be fairly soon. Give her a present, perhaps . . . she'd done her best to be pleasant and sympathetic towards him, encouraging him to talk. She meant well, no doubt, but he had felt even more wretched afterwards, knowing how much he had left unsaid, and how much he could not bear to confront, even in his own thoughts. She was very sweet, and had done her best; she would have done far more if he had permitted it, he knew. That night she had come into his room, he had come dangerously close to forgetting how young she was, and that he was a guest in her parents' house, honour-bound to behave properly. He had taken care that such a situation did not arise again, knowing that it would be all too easy to surrender himself to his instincts . . . might, in fact, be the very thing he needed . . .

But for now there was tonight to be got through. Andrew would probably be at Mullaghcleevaun already, acting as if he couldn't imagine how the house had functioned without him, casting his damned superior glances at everyone. A cold fish, Andrew, the type who did well in the army . . . His Mention in Despatches, as far as Uncle Douglas was concerned, made the whole war worthwhile – "showed coolness, and complete disregard for his personal safety" . . . Easy enough to be brave, if you've no imagination . . .

Of all people, Martin did not want to meet Andrew.

Sparks

Catherine spent a long time getting ready for dinner. When she had pinned up her hair to her satisfaction she checked her appearance in front of the long mirror. The new dress fitted well, she decided; it showed off her figure without restricting her movements. Against the silky lilac fabric, her skin looked pale and her eyes large. Making a final adjustment to an errant strand of hair, she wondered momentarily for whose benefit she had taken such trouble. Martin would take no notice of her; she would probably be seated near Maura at dinner, her mother not having noticed their quarrel, and Maura certainly wasn't going to be interested in feminine fripperies. Conor, the only person she might have liked to impress, wouldn't even see her. Besides, she had a feeling that he would prefer her in white-wash-spattered overalls.

She went downstairs, infected in spite of herself by the party atmosphere. Cocktails were being served in the drawing room, and her father forgot himself so far as to mix her a glass. Andrew was chatting to Christopher Delaunay about the recent municipal elections, while Martin, politely attentive, stood in a corner with Mrs Delaunay, who seemed to be telling him about the Wimbledon tennis tournament. Even Aunt Madge had been invited to make a rare appearance; her presence at the dinner table was usually limited to Christmas Day, Easter Sunday and family birthdays. Social occasions tired her, and Catherine knew that she would be taken back upstairs by Phyllis as soon as dinner was over. She always wore the same dress, a Victorian-looking garment of heavy black lace, encrusted with beads of jet. Silver and pearl earrings dangled incongruously at each side of her withered neck, and her thin hair was held back by jewelled tortoiseshell combs. She sat, very upright, in a wing-backed chair, from which she surveyed the room imperiously. Catherine almost expected to see two or three cats peeping out from under her skirts or sleeping in her black lace lap.

Catherine greeted the Fitzwilliams rather guardedly, and went over to her great-aunt. "Good evening, Aunt Madge. How are the cats?"

The old lady's blue eyes focused on the cocktail glass in Catherine's hand. "You shouldn't be drinking at your age. When's Edwin coming?"

"I don't know," Catherine said. She had meant to ask her mother who this mysterious Edwin was. She hoped that Aunt Madge would manage to keep at least some hold on reality, not spend the evening talking to people who weren't there.

At that moment, all eyes were drawn to the doorway where Celeste Fraser was making her entrance. She wore a sheath-like dress diagonally striped in blue and scarlet, flashing with brilliants, and an ebony bangle coiled up one bare arm like a snake. Her dark hair was brushed as close to her head as a swimming cap, with a curl teased forward in front of each ear. Behind her, her husband Simon looked insignificant, and she made all the other women appear drab in their more restrained finery. Catherine was amused by the various reactions, from the colonel's sharp intake of breath so that he almost choked on his drink, to Delia's envious, "Darling, how simply dashing. Where did you get that dress?" Catherine looked automatically towards Martin, to gauge his response. Although his gaze rested on Celeste appraisingly, she sensed that he did not really approve, that Celeste was not the kind of woman he admired. But why should she care what he thought, she rebuked herself? It made no difference. And perhaps the evening would turn out to be fun after all; Celeste certainly looked as if she had every intention of livening things up.

The dining table had been extended to its full length to take fourteen people (a bachelor acquaintance of the colonel's, Mr Loosemore, had been invited to make the numbers work out), and it was set with the best damask napkins and cut glass, and bowls of roses from the garden, which filled the air with their perfume. Martin, taking his seat between Maura and Aunt Madge, gave Catherine a wry smile; conversation at that corner of the table was likely to be limited. But, as it happened, an innocuous exchange between Mrs Delaunay and Celeste during the fish course set the tone for most of the meal.

"Is this your first visit to Ireland, Mrs Fraser?"

"Yes, it is," Celeste replied. "I must say it isn't quite the hotbed of revolution we were expecting from the London papers. We were half-afraid we'd be attacked by gun-toting Fenians before we got out of Kingstown, weren't we, Simon? I suppose the rumours are exaggerated?"

"Well . . ." Mrs Delaunay hesitated, and Catherine remembered the manservant who had been killed.

"Possibly," Mr Delaunay said, "but the fact is that one's never sure what will happen next. We owe our security to people like Major Enright here." He nodded towards Andrew.

"What is your job, exactly, Andrew?" Celeste asked. "I don't have to call you Major, do I?"

Andrew shook his head. "I'm in army intelligence, based at Dublin Castle."

"So your post is directly concerned with the sort of thing we've been reading about?" Celeste asked him. "Trying to prevent the shootings and roadblocks and so on?"

"Something of that sort, yes."

"And will you get the situation under control," Celeste persisted, "now that these troops from England have been brought in?"

"I imagine so," Andrew said curtly. "But it's a dirty, underhand business. The Auxiliaries and the RIC, going about their business in uniform, are at the mercy of any hooligan who can get his hands on a gun, and thinks he turns himself into a hero for Ireland by taking a pot-shot from behind a hedge."

"Terrible state of affairs," the colonel said.

"But surely you can't approve of the Black and Tans, the way they've been behaving?" Maura said. Her clear voice from the other end of the table silenced the murmurs of other conversations. "From what I've heard, they're just as bad as the hooligans you criticise."

Andrew gave her an aloof smile. "I daresay the rumours on that subject are wildly exaggerated."

"What do you think will be the outcome?" Simon Fraser asked Andrew.

"Oh, they'll get their Home Rule." Andrew paused to drain his wine glass. "And a sorry thing it will be for all of us. The country will be in the hands of a bunch of gunmen, with no experience of anything except rabble-rousing. What will happen then is anyone's guess. The irony of it is that Home Rule was on the statute book as long ago as before the war. They'd have got it anyway, without that ridiculous business back in '16, and all the brouhaha now."

Bridie, her face expressionless, was removing the fish plates. Catherine wondered what she thought of the fragments of conversation she overheard, and whether she repeated them in the kitchen. Most adults of her acquaintance treated servants as if they were deaf and dumb, as well as invisible, but now she remembered the RIC sergeant's visit, and thought of the unknown girl, Mary, in the kitchen. Andrew had warned her about talking to the servants, but surely talking in front of them was much the same thing.

"Isn't that the point?" Maura leaned forward, rising to the challenge. Catherine noticed Mrs Fitzwilliam darting an apologetic look at Delia, embarrassed by her daughter's vehemence. Girls were not expected to venture opinions on politics. "The whole point," Maura repeated, "is that nothing's changed since the war, in spite of Irish contribution to the war effort. All those deaths, on Gallipoli and the Somme and in Flanders . . . and what does the British government do but try to introduce conscription in Ireland? And still Home Rule's being delayed, and still it means partition. Can you really be surprised that it's not enough?"

"I agree with Maura," Martin joined in. "The Irish have always been treated abominably, and there seems to be no change in that respect."

Andrew picked up his wine glass, realised that there was nothing in it and gave Martin a hostile look across the table. Maura glanced at Martin too, evidently surprised by his unexpected support. Everyone had now been served with plates of steaming beef, and Bridie came round to offer vegetables.

"When's Edwin coming?" Aunt Madge's voice rose plaintively. "There's no place at the table for Edwin."

"Hush, dear." The colonel patted her hand. "We'll find a place for Edwin if he comes."

"I see," Andrew said, still looking at Martin. "So you think we should forget about Home Rule – simply clear out and hand over the country to the mob? What do you imagine would happen then, to people like ourselves? It's all right for you, I suppose – you could go straight back home, but what would you recommend we do with Mullaghcleevaun, for instance? Hand it over as a gift to the Irish Republic?"

"I don't see that the situation need be as extreme as that," Martin said. "Why shouldn't there be room for Protestants as well as Catholics in an independent Ireland?"

Andrew smiled complacently. "That remark, if you'll pardon my saying so, Martin, could only come from someone who has no idea what the situation is really like in this country."

"Perhaps an outsider doesn't share your preconceptions," Martin replied. "Protestants and Catholics live together amicably enough in other countries."

Catherine found herself speaking up. "I think the Anglo-Irish in this country try to pretend that nothing's going to change because they – I mean we – don't want it to." She felt rather pleased to have been able to contribute, before realising that she had been quoting Conor.

Andrew, however, ignored her, and replied to Martin, "As I said just now, that simply shows how little you understand. There's more to it than religious differences."

"Major Enright has a point, of course," Christopher Delaunay said smoothly. "The more extreme element won't be content with Home Rule now – they want complete independence, an Irish Republic. And clearly the British government isn't going to agree to that, especially if the Republicans are going to use violence to try to get it."

"What else is there for them to do?" Maura said. "Haven't the past few years shown that political campaigning doesn't work? And that the British government will keep Irish nationalists hanging on, and hanging on, and then give them as little as it can, with a divided country into the bargain?"

"What you don't seem to understand, Maura," Andrew said, with infuriating calm, "is that the Republicans are in a tiny minority. Most Irish people would be perfectly content with Home Rule. That was proved back in '16, when the rebels were looked on as a bunch of madmen."

"Until the leaders were executed," Christopher Delaunay remarked drily. "That probably got them more sympathy than a successful rebellion would have done."

"Yes, and doesn't that just show the maudlin sentimentality of the Irish mind," Andrew retorted, raising his newly filled glass. "A man's a half-witted hothead until he's dead, and then he instantly becomes a martyr, ranked alongside St Patrick, I shouldn't wonder."

"And I suppose you think people feel about the victims of the Black and Tans with the same maudlin sentimentality?" Maura said crushingly. "Have any of the Tans ever been brought to justice for the crimes they've committed?"

"Crimes? I'm afraid I don't quite see how doing one's best to maintain law and order, against all the odds, can be regarded as a criminal offence."

Catherine noticed her mother's tight expression and knew that she was unhappy about the way her dinner party was going. Politics was one of the topics conventionally not raised at the table; some of the other diners were looking uncomfortable, Patsy's tender roast beef had gone unremarked, and Maura had hardly touched the food on her plate.

"Hush, Maura! I think you've made your point," Mrs Fitzwilliam reproved. Maura began to pick at her food, although Catherine sensed that there was a good deal more she would have liked to say. She and Andrew were like flints striking sparks off each other, for all that their argument had been conducted beneath a veneer of civility. She was aware of a grudging admiration for Maura, feeling instinctively that her views were more valid than Andrew's. Maura had thought about the issue from both sides, while Andrew was only justifying his own position.

"Do let's talk about something else," Delia

said sweetly. "Another glass of wine, Mr Loosemore? Bridie, fill Mr Loosemore's glass."

"You young people are idealists, of course," Mr Fitzwilliam said, regardless. "That's right and proper. But when you've lived in Ireland as long as I have you'll see that it isn't a matter of simple right and wrong. There are infinite complications. It takes experience to understand."

His remark, vague and patronising though it was, brought the discussion to a close. Catherine, aware that he had lumped herself, Martin and Maura together as youthful idealists, thought how ironic it was that all three of them had been at odds before this evening. Now, Maura caught her eye across the table and gave a faint exasperated sigh, as if acknowledging her as an ally.

"Mr and Mrs Fraser are keen golfers," Delia said to the Delaunays, in an obvious attempt to steer the conversation elsewhere.

At the other end of the table Aunt Madge took hold of Martin's sleeve and asked him whether he had seen anything of dear Clarissa while he was out in India. Celeste, looking rather taken aback by the strength of feeling her remarks had unwittingly stirred up, rose to the occasion by giving a spirited account of her disaster at the tenth hole; before long a more light-hearted mood was regained, and Patsy's flans and decorated fruit moulds received due appreciation.

When the meal was over, and everyone had retired to the drawing room, Maura was encouraged by Delia to play the piano, and Celeste pulled her husband to his feet to partner her in a waltz. The Delaunays followed suit, and then Delia held out her hand to Martin, who obligingly stood up. Catherine, unreasonably put out by this, was asked to dance by the middle-aged Mr Loosemore, who held her stiffly at arm's length as if she were a fragile piece of cut glass, and looked steadfastly over her shoulder the whole time, not speaking. She half-closed her eyes so that she could replace him with a more attractive imaginary partner, and thought about dancing with Conor, his arms holding her more closely than Mr Loosemore's, his green eyes looking into hers, the way he had looked at her in the woods that night ... The music ended, and she opened her eyes to see Mr Loosemore's grey face instead of Conor's tanned one; he bowed very formally and thanked her. Maura selected a new piece, and then Martin came over and said, "Will you dance this one with me, Catherine?" and held out his arms to her.

Maura started to play. Catherine instantly forgot her annoyance with Martin over the last few days, and that she had only just been day-dreaming about Conor, and thought of nothing except dancing with Martin. His hand was firm and warm in hers as he guided her easily among the other dancers, whose presence had all but faded from her consciousness. He smiled at her as he whirled her round, and she thought how beautifully the black evening jacket and stiff white collar suited him, and how well he moved, his body close but not touching hers, and how dark his eyes were ... She was appalled by her capriciousness, but it was hopeless even trying to resist; her feelings refused to be bound by reason. She couldn't help it. She loved them both, Conor and Martin, both of them at once, and there was nothing she could do to stop herself. She saw Maura glancing in their direction as she played, and she knew that Maura had read her feelings as plainly as if they were written in the air above her head. But she couldn't hide it, not with the combination of the wine, and the soft lighting, and Martin smiling at her.

And then, too soon, the waltz reached its final chord. Martin gave a bow and said, "Thank you, Catherine," and led her back to her seat, and it was over.

Maura was turning the pages of the music-book, selecting another piece, but Celeste called out, "Let Simon play for a while, Maura. It isn't fair for you to miss all the dancing."

"I don't mind," Maura said.

"No, really. Come and dance," Celeste insisted.

Maura stood up, offering Simon the book of waltzes, but he shook his head and settled himself on the stool, putting the book aside. He exchanged a glance with Celeste and then spread his fingers over the keys and began to play, not another stately waltz but a jazz piece, swaying his body to its pulsing rhythm. Those guests who had been standing poised for another waltz or foxtrot looked at each other in consternation, not sure how to dance to it.

"Come on, Martin. Won't you dance?" Celeste stretched out her hand to him where he stood by the window. Martin hesitated, but was too polite to refuse, and Catherine sensed that he didn't know how to dance to the jazz music either. Celeste took him in an exaggerated ballroom hold, elbows out, head turned sharply to the right, and began to move in time to the energetic rhythm, quick-stepping, legs and back stiff. Martin, looking self-conscious, did his best to match his movements to hers. Celeste laughed at him, enjoying his awkwardness and her own skilled performance. No one else had joined in, and all the other guests looked on, while Simon quickened the rhythm to force the dancers to an even more frenetic pace. When the music reached its final jangling chords, Martin looked mightily relieved, escaping quickly to a smattering of applause from the audience. Simon launched immediately into another jaunty piece, and this time Celeste commandeered a reluctant Mr Loosemore, while Delia dragged Mr Fitzwilliam to his feet.

"Come on then, Catherine," Andrew said. "We may as well make ourselves look ridiculous."

Martin went over to Maura, who stood up looking as if she considered this sort of thing to be beneath her. Andrew, to Catherine's surprise, was rather good at this eccentric style of dancing, and she began to enjoy herself, loosening her limbs to the syncopated rhythm; it was far more fun than the conventional waltzes, where you had to remember to be graceful and try to avoid treading on your partner's toes. By the end of the piece, all the dancers looked flushed with heat and exertion. Delia, fanning herself, said, "We'd better have something a little more restful, don't you think, before trying this again?"

The colonel opened some windows, letting in a drift of cool air, and Simon obliged by rippling his fingers over the piano keys as a prelude to the most soothing of waltzes. Catherine's gyrations had loosened a skein of her hair, so that she felt cold pins slithering down the back of her dress. Excusing herself from Andrew, she went upstairs to her room to repair the damage.

Her face in the bedroom mirror looked pink and hot, far from the sophisticated image she had imagined herself to be presenting. When she had rearranged her hair she washed her face at the basin and dabbed it dry on a towel. Then she turned off her bedroom light and went out on to the landing. Suddenly wanting to be alone with her confused feelings for a little longer, she opened the window to let the air cool her cheeks. A half-moon was rising in the twilight, silvering the edges of low streamers of cloud, touching the surface of the pond with light. The night smelled warmly of cut grass and breathing foliage, with a faint tang of sea air carried on the breeze. At the end of the garden, the woods looked black, impenetrable to the failing light, guarding their secrets of forbidden poaching and forbidden love. As Catherine's eyes adjusted to the half-light, she looked towards the gardener's cottage, thinking of Conor with a pang of guilt. Had he been working there this evening? She hoped not. She felt ashamed, not liking the possibility that she had been dining, and drinking wine, and wallowing in stupid thoughts about Martin, while he had been working there alone. Her eye caught a faint movement in the bushes beside the cottage, and she narrowed her eyes and tried to make out whatever had caused it. Surely Conor could not still be there, even if he had been working earlier? It was almost too dark to see.

After a few moments she decided that it must have been a cat or a fox moving through the undergrowth. Leaving the window open, she went downstairs, already hoping that Martin would ask her to dance again.

Concealed by the elder bushes beside the gardener's cottage, the gunman waited.

Another half-hour or so, he reckoned, and he'd give up; it didn't look as if the long-awaited opportunity would arise after all. It would be more difficult if he had to get into the house later, but he would do it. It would make little difference to his victim: a few glasses of champagne more or less, a few more dances, to judge from the sounds of jollity drifting across the lawn, and the shadows of moving figures against the curtains; either way, the execution would be carried out. He tightened his grip on the army service rifle which had served him so well since its theft from a barracks in Cork six weeks ago, lovingly smoothing a hand along its barrels. The irony of using this particular weapon for the job pleased him.

Ten minutes or so later the front door of the house opened, throwing a lozenge of light across the porch, and a figure in a dark evening suit emerged. The gunman, who had watched the guests arriving, knew that there was no one else in the house of similar age and build; luck was on his side tonight after all. He caught his breath, raising the rifle slowly into position.

His intended target walked slowly across the lawn, looking down at the grass. Reaching the pond, he stepped on to the low humped bridge and stood fumbling in his pockets. He placed a cigarette in his mouth and then a struck match flared and he cupped his hand to light up, his silhouette blackly defined against the moon-glinting water.

The gunman had him clearly in his sights.

"Enjoy your smoke, Major Enright, you bastard," he muttered under his breath.

Slowly walking down the stairs, Catherine paused as she saw a pair of black-trousered legs and feet in patent leather shoes cross to the front doormat, the rest of the figure hidden from view by the farther edge of the stairwell. She heard the front door open, and when she reached the entrance hall she saw that it had been left ajar.

Familiar with Andrew's habit of going outside after dinner on summer evenings to smoke a cigar, she glanced out of the door as she passed, and then saw from the slighter build and dejected walk that it was not Andrew after all, but Martin.

She slipped out of the door and stood in the shadows beside the porch, watching him. His abrupt changes of mood baffled and intrigued her. He had been coping well this evening – challenging Andrew at dinner, dancing, being sociable – but now, as so often, he apparently felt the need to withdraw, to retreat into his own thoughts. She could picture the expression she knew so well by now: tight-lipped, dark eyes clouded and downcast . . . As always, when he lapsed into one of these moods, she had to resist the urge to go after him, to ask him what was in his mind. He reached the ornamental bridge, and stood there motionless, smoking. A scene unreeled itself in her mind like the climax to some sentimental film: she would go to him, and he would turn to her on the bridge and take her in his arms and tell her that he loved her, and the violins would soar and the moon rise overhead, and they would kiss passionately, silhouetted against the water. But cold common sense intervened enough to make her realise that he was just as likely to tell her to leave him alone and stop being a nuisance.

It occurred to her how foolish she would look if anyone came out of the house and found her gazing after him in that soppy way. She ought to go back to the dancing.

And then she saw something pale on the bridge, close to Martin's feet. One of Aunt Madge's cats . . . Martin stooped to stroke it. At that instant a loud crack resounded across the lawn, startling Catherine almost out of her wits, and the cat streaked across the grass while Martin crumpled up and slowly toppled into the water.

Martin

Catherine screamed.

The rifle shot had shattered the evening into fragments, the whipcrack echoing in her ears along with her own piercing cry. Her legs swayed beneath her and she clutched at the stonework of the porch for support, afraid she would lose consciousness. Then figures erupted from the hallway and she clutched wildly at the first person she saw.

"They've killed him . . ."

Delia's face contorted. "Oh, my God – they've shot Andrew – "

"No, not Andrew . . ." Catherine's head reeled. "Martin . . . in the pond . . ."

She pulled at her mother's arm, and Andrew appeared in the porch, behind the others, his face white and startled. He took charge instantly.

"Martin? My God – go and fetch him, Dad – be careful – Simon, Christopher, come with me. There are revolvers in the study. Mother, phone the police and a doctor. Stay here with the women," he added to Mr Loosemore. "Did anyone see what happened?"

"Catherine did . . ."

"Catherine, did you see where the shot came from?"

"From the cottage," Catherine gasped. Her mind refused to grapple with the implications. She forced her shaking legs to carry her, to break into a run after her father. Behind, people seemed to be dashing everywhere, pushing past each other. Somehow her legs carried her across the grass. Her shocked brain repeated, "They've killed Martin. Martin's dead, in the pond," but the words refused to register.

"The bridge," she gasped as she stumbled forward. "He fell off the bridge."

Celeste was there first, running ahead with agile strides. The water glimmered darkly. They should have brought torches, Catherine thought; they'd never find him. But there was a dark shape, floating, and Celeste kicked off her shoes and plunged straight in, up to her thighs in water. She grabbed hold of the motionless black shape which was Martin and hauled him over so that his face was uppermost. Then she lost her footing on the mud bottom and sat down, almost disappearing beneath the pond weed and lily leaves. Trying to regain her presence of mind, Catherine threw off her own shoes and waded in after her,

224

the water dragging at her skirt, cold mud oozing through her stockings. Between them they hauled Martin to the edge, and Maura and the colonel reached down to drag him clear of the water. He was surprisingly heavy, his body limp and weighed down by saturated clothes.

Celeste unfastened his collar and then rolled him face down and began to apply artificial respiration.

What's the point? Catherine thought numbly. He's dead, he's been shot, not drowned. She was too numb to weep.

Maura, more practical, lifted one of Martin's arms, unfastening the cuff-links, pressing her fingers against his wrist.

"There's a pulse. A very faint one, but I can feel it."

Catherine, a faint hope leaping, thought Maura must be mistaken. "There must be a wound . . . I saw him fall. He bent down . . . there was a cat . . ."

Celeste sat back on her heels and bent her head down, close to Martin's. "I think he's breathing, but I can't see what else . . ." Her fingers ran gently through Martin's hair, and then she said, "It's here, I think. I can feel blood. We'd better get him indoors. We can't do anything here, not even see how bad it is."

Mr Loosemore ran down the lawn to help.

Everyone lifted an arm or a leg and they carried Martin up to the house, as carefully as possible. His face in the indoor light was white, with a long trickle of blood down one cheek. Catherine's appalled eyes took in his pallor and the slow stain spreading over his shirt collar. His eyes were turned up under almost-closed lids, showing only the whites; there was no flicker of movement. Oh, God, Catherine thought, he had retained this fragile hold on life only to die from his wound . . . she couldn't bear it. Not half an hour ago she had been dancing with him . . . The older women fussed round, and Mrs Fitzwilliam was in tears. Catherine was thankful for Celeste's calm efficiency, the last person she would have expected to exhibit such a quality in a crisis. Celeste had been a nurse in the war, she remembered gratefully.

Martin was lain down on one of the drawing-room sofas. Someone fetched blankets, and Celeste examined the wound and said to Delia, "Bring some lint, could you, or some handkerchieves? How long is the doctor likely to take?"

Her stunning dress was ruined, streaked with mud, a few strands of bright-green waterweed clinging to the coloured beads. There was a smell of dank pond-slime, and Catherine looked down at her own soaked dress and muddy feet and shivered. Celeste glanced at her and said, "Catherine, you ought to sit down. Can someone get her a blanket and a hot drink? She must be suffering from shock."

"But Martin – " Catherine did not want to leave him.

"I don't think this is as bad as it looks," Celeste said. "Scalp wounds bleed like nobody's business."

Catherine succumbed to being sat down in an armchair and wrapped in a blanket as if she were a baby. Her numb mind attempted to recall the salient facts of the incident. Martin was alive, but someone had tried to kill him, and doubtless would have succeeded if it hadn't been for Aunt Madge's cat . . . Patsy brought her a mug of hot cocoa and she clasped her chilled fingers around it.

Why would anyone want to kill Martin? . . . And then she remembered her mother's instinctive reaction, and knew that the bullet had been intended not for Martin, but for Andrew. And the rifle had been fired from the gardener's cottage. She remembered the movement she had seen earlier from the upstairs window, and knew that she could have saved Martin if only she had been more alert, if her head had been less fuddled with wine and stupid romantic yearnings.

She pictured the gunman waiting there for Andrew, and her imagination supplied an identity. In spite of the blanket and the hot drink, she shivered.

"Quite frankly, as you say he's already been getting over some nervous disorder, I'd recommend that he stays here," Doctor Feeney said, replacing his hat. "It would be far less traumatic for him to regain consciousness in familiar surroundings. Call me as soon as he comes round. You'll make sure someone stays with him?"

"Of course," Delia said.

"The wound itself shouldn't cause complications now that I've stitched it. He was very lucky, from what you say." The doctor nodded at Catherine. "The bullet grazed the scalp, with no obvious damage to the skull. I'll carry out further tests when he's conscious."

The doctor left, and Delia locked and bolted the door behind him and pulled the heavy velvet curtain over it as if it were mid-winter. Catherine watched her, certain that they would never again feel safe in their own home. The guests had all gone now, apart from the Frasers, who were having a calming drink in the drawing room. Andrew had stayed upstairs with Martin.

"It was meant for Andrew, wasn't it?" Catherine said.

"We can only suppose so." Delia looked as if she were about to cry. "We should have been more careful. We didn't want to admit it was a possibility. We thought we were immune."

Andrew and the other men had found no trace of the would-be assassin when they had gone out to investigate, and neither had the RIC.

"It's hopeless, with all these trees," Andrew had said. "An intruder could slip away in several different directions. The worrying thing is that it's obviously someone who knows the area very well – probably they've been sneaking around for some while."

Catherine would not tell them what she suspected. She would have to face up to that by herself.

Hell's Gate

Martin had been looking in puzzlement at the slumped figure for several minutes, trying to work out what the hell Andrew was doing in his bedroom in the middle of the night. Andrew was dozing in an upright chair, his shoulders sagging to one side and his head lolling. And then his head swung further under its own weight and jolted him awake. He blinked in confusion, and his eyes focused on Martin's face and he jumped again.

"Good Lord! You're awake! How long have you been lying there like that?"

"Not long." Martin lifted his head to speak and was conscious of a pounding ache in his temples. A hand raised to his forehead met with a stiff padding of bandages.

"Steady on . . ." Andrew stood up and bent over him solicitously. "How do you feel? Do you remember what happened?"

"Yes, I think so. Something hit me . . ." He was going to say a sniper, but then he remembered that he was at Mullaghcleevaun, not in Flanders.

"Someone took a shot at you. You had a lucky escape, just a scalp wound, the doctor says. Look, will you be all right if I leave you for a minute or two? You won't pass out again, or anything? Doctor Feeney said we had to call him straight away, whatever time it was."

"I'll be all right," Martin said, and Andrew went out.

He lay back again, staring at the ceiling which was dimly lit by a greyish dawn light. His head reeled slightly and he could feel the soreness of his scalp now, as well as the headache. He thought about what Andrew had said. He could remember quite clearly the few moments on the bridge: lighting a cigarette, that cat stalking up and rubbing itself against his legs, and then the mind-jolting crack. It all seemed rather unimportant, like something he had watched in a film or seen happening to someone else. Stupid, really, he thought, remembering all the times he'd got himself into a cold funk over nothing more sinister than a roadside ditch or a line of trees. Now that someone really had taken a pot-shot at him he found that he could contemplate it quite calmly. Plenty of people were getting shot at in Ireland just now; why should he be any different? It was not worth getting agitated about. Meanwhile, the pain in his head faded gradually into a floating sensation which was not unpleasant, rather like the effects of the wine and cocktails last night.

He had been perhaps half an inch from death, he thought dispassionately. What difference would it have made? He should have been dead by now anyway; he should have died with Panton. The memory was still there, no matter how hard he tried to suppress it.

The other second-lieutenant had told Martin that it was bad luck to be sent to the Ypres salient, his first time out; every experienced soldier dreaded it. Martin, having been sent up to replace a junior officer killed by a stray shell a few days earlier, was one of the few members of the Company who hadn't been in that section before – hadn't been in any part of the front line. Bailleul, the busy rail-head town where Martin's unit was billeted before moving up, struck him as a kind of departure point for the Underworld; troops returning from Zonnebeke and Brood-seinde – the names already rang ominously in Martin's ears – were haggard, gaunt-eyed, mud-plastered, too exhausted to speak. A few days in the pleasant cafés and estaminets of Bailleul would go some way towards reviving them, but Martin had seen the dispirited, fatalistic

232

expression on the faces of columns moving back into the trenches, and he dreaded the inevitable orders to proceed up the line. The other second-lieutenant was called Overstone, an amiable blond youth of about his own age. Martin did not ask him what it would be like up there. He would find out soon enough.

A few days later the Company advanced to Zonnebeke. From there, Overstone told Martin, they would be strengthening an advance to capture a village called Passchendaele. The Messines Ridge, to the south, had been captured back in June, around the time of Martin's and Serena's Wrekin walk; he had read of the "Brilliant British Success" in the newspapers in the following days, and he could still remember how appropriate it had seemed, part of his sense that everything was going well for him, the war as well as his personal life. It seemed a very long time ago now, an incredibly naïve thing to have thought. There was not much to be optimistic about here.

The aim was to follow through this victory by pushing forward and straightening out the bulge in the front line around the medieval city of Ypres. Grandiose plans of sweeping straight on to Ostend and Zeebrugge had been forgotten, and the objective now was a small insignificant village separated from Ypres by a few bleak miles. Both armies were stuck in the mud, Overstone said.

This was a masterly understatement, as Martin soon saw. Ravaged villages, blackened stumps of trees, cottages smashed into heaps of brick – these were familiar sights from the march up from Bailleul, but nothing had prepared him for the Salient itself. The marshy terrain had been turned to quagmire by heavy rain, the drainage ditches smashed by prolonged shelling. Martin's eyes swept over an ocean of mud, shell-holes brimming with oily water, tree-stumps like rotted teeth, and the crumbled remains of dwellings. He could not imagine how they were supposed to survive in this, let alone fight. He thought bitterly of the model trenches he had seen at Officers' Training Camp – perfectly maintained, with revetments and firing-steps and parapets, and cosy dugouts carved out of the sides. Nothing like that here. Lengths of duckboard zigzagged about as if in some bizarre game of snakes and ladders, making it hard to imagine that a proper trench system existed. At night, the whole scene was weirdly illuminated by the soaring star-shells and the greenish light of flares, recalling medieval paintings of hell.

Men lived for days at a time here in the inadequate trenches and soggy dugouts, damp, cold and miserable. Martin was supposed to present his platoon for stand-to, and supervise the rebuilding of parapets and the baling of water and the replacing of duckboards, and organise sentries. No orders came for the rumoured attack, but the waiting was even worse. Martin felt that the stench of decomposing flesh pervaded his whole body, polluting the air he breathed and reaching to every cell and capillary and nerve ending. He thought of Serena sometimes, as someone who had existed in a distant, irretrievable dream. Her photograph was in his wallet, but he would not take it out to look at it, for fear that he would contaminate her with filth.

After two weeks alternating between the front line and the support trenches, they went back to farm billets, where a few days of parading and drilling and kit inspection were intended to restore morale. Martin shared a comfortable room in the eaves with Overstone, where at least he was warm and dry. But he could not escape the isolated horrors which reappeared in his dreams. A disembodied hand stretching out of a water-filled shell-hole . . . the carcase of a horse bloated and filled with gas . . . fragments of human corpse built into the parapet, but slithering out with each fresh fall of rain . . . And yet by now such sights had become commonplace.

He had not been in an attack yet, and he knew he would not be able to stand it. He almost hoped to be killed in the first few minutes, so that his ordeal would be over. While they were in the farmhouse Overstone spent his free time writing letters home, or trying to get Martin to play cards with him, or strolling about the orchard, whistling cheerfully. He was eminently likeable, but Martin sometimes hated him for his stoical acceptance of whatever Fate, or senior command, brought them. If only Overstone would say, "I can't face the thought of going back up the line," or "I don't think I can stick another advance," Martin would have felt less inadequate. But Overstone never complained, as if this were his natural way of life and he expected nothing better.

When the advance came, Martin had already been reduced to incoherent terror by the preliminary bombardment. The heavy guns were positioned well back and the shells overhead ripped through the sky like claws, the ground quaking to their thunder. The noise deafened, leaving no room for rational thought, no room even for sanity. Martin clasped his hands to his ears and closed his eyes, trying vainly to shut it all out. At last the bombardment dwindled and stopped, yet the oppressive silence was even worse, pressing against his ears until he thought their drums would cave in. Overstone, nearest to Martin, kept his face to the sagging parapet, waiting to go over. And then whistles sounded and Overstone scrambled up. Martin had forgotten that he was supposed to blow his own whistle and wave on his platoon; he followed Overstone blindly, desperate to keep close to his heels as if the other lieutenant could somehow protect him. Retaliatory shells whined over to explode in the water-filled craters, sending great fountains of sludge over the advancing troops. Men ahead of Martin screamed and threw up their arms as they fell, so that as he crawled forward he had to avoid writhing, contorted bodies ... A shell screamed, and he buried his face in his arms, pressing himself into the mud as if trying to drown himself in it. It was in his nose, his eyes, he could taste it in his mouth ... Splinters sprayed down, and he heard whimpering and realised that he was not alone in his extremity of fear; someone near him had crawled into a shell-hole to cling there, sobbing. Martin crawled closer and recognised the white, stricken face of Panton, a boy from his platoon. Glad of the excuse not to keep going, Martin scrambled towards him, legs sinking.

"Are you hit?" he shouted.

Panton stared at him with bulging, bloodshot eyes, and Martin knew that the boy was as terrified as he was himself.

"Panton, it's me, Sheringham," he shouted

again. "Are you hit?" He grasped the boy's shoulder and shook it.

"No . . . n-no, sir," Panton stammered. "But I can't go on, I can't . . ." He was weeping like a child, his shoulders shaking.

Martin knew that he should urge Panton to his feet, and bully him into getting on with it, as Captain Waverley would undoubtedly have done, threatening him with his revolver if necessary. Above all, he ought to press forward himself. But he did nothing, except allow Panton to go on sobbing. If they waited a little longer, the troops farther ahead would draw most of the enemy fire, and the shells would be falling shorter. It would be easy enough to catch up later, when the shelling was less ferocious . . .

"Come on," he said to Panton, when at last he judged it safe enough to proceed. Panton whimpered and protested, and Martin had to grab him by the elbow and pull him. He crawled to the lip of the shell-hole. The air was full of smoke and the acrid smell of cordite. A few shapes loomed ahead in the haze, but apart from that there was only the ratatat of machine-gun fire to indicate which way was forward. Martin realised that he had been left behind more successfully than he had intended. Unless a chance shell over-reached, the danger had passed them by, the wave of the advance had swept over them. The shell-craters were so close together here that it was easy enough to creep from one to the next, rarely appearing above ground level. And then, slithering over a muddy ridge, Martin came face to face with a floating corpse and gave an involuntary yell of fright. A stain hung darkly in the green water and the white grimacing face was uppermost, its wide-open eyes fixing Martin with what seemed to be a stare of accusation. A wave of nausea gripped him, and Panton, clinging to his legs, burst into fresh sobs.

"I can't go on, sir, I can't!"

"You've got to . . ."

But the young private was becoming hysterical, turning his face away, choking. In despair, Martin thought he would have to leave him. He hauled the resisting boy away from the corpse.

"You'll have to come with me."

"Don't make me, sir, I said don't . . ." Panton's teeth clenched in childish anger and he stood up, flinging Martin away from him with unexpected strength. Sprawling in the mud, Martin watched helplessly as Panton tried to run, skidding, falling over, picking himself up again and stumbling on. Martin had no idea which direction he was aiming for, or whether he had any idea at all. But there was no more Martin could do. He had to think of himself.

Now he was confused as to which way the

advance had gone. Shells were exploding fitfully
now, like a thunderstorm fading into the distance, and the rattle of machine-gun fire was
deceptive, one moment sounding close at hand,
the next minute a hundred yards or so to his
right. The only figures to be seen were dead
bodies, skewed into unnatural postures. Carefully avoiding them, Martin picked his way
round the shell-craters, trying to look purposeful
in case anyone came across him. After a while he
crossed some battered remains of barbed wire
and looked down in astonishment to find himself
on the lip of a trench, a trench far deeper and
better constructed than any he had seen since
training camp, and one which appeared to be
unoccupied. He jumped down into it, grateful
for the cover, and then saw a slumped figure in
Prussian grey, with the distinctive coal-scuttle
helmet, and realised with a tremor of disbelief
that he was in the German front line. He bent
down to examine the dead German, who had
apparently been killed by shell-splinters, and as
he did so a rifle barrel prodded him and he jerked
upright to meet the approving gaze of another
officer from his company, Lieutenant Keene.

"Well done, Sheringham. You must have been
well ahead. We'll consolidate this section. Are
any of your platoon with you?"

"I lost sight of them in the shelling," Martin mumbled.

"There are some stragglers coming in now. Send a group into the next fire-bay – make sure they've got plenty of grenades. Then we'll get these machine-gun posts turned round."

Keene took charge, and Martin did his best to appear efficient, amazed at his undeserved luck. When the new stretch of line was occupied, sentries posted and the dugouts checked, Captain Waverley came round to inspect their position, and congratulated the two junior officers on their achievement.

"Sheringham here must take the credit," Keene said generously. "He seems to have captured the trench single-handed."

Martin muttered something suitably modest, without disillusioning Keene. If Captain Waverley had his suspicions, he did not voice them. But later, when Panton had been court-martialled and sentenced, and Waverley told Martin that he had to command the firing squad, Martin wondered whether he had guessed at the truth, or part of it. The night before they came out of the line, Waverley was wounded by a sniper's bullet whilst out on a wiring party; he was sent down to a Casualty Clearing Station, and Martin never saw him again.

Overstone had been killed in the advance.

When Panton was led out to face his execution, he was not weeping, but resigned. Briefly wondering whether the boy welcomed this end rather than face another bombardment and advance, Martin realised that this was merely a palliative to his own guilty feelings. Panton recognised Martin in the few moments before the blindfold was bound in place, and his eyes rested on Martin's face without malice or resentment, simply expressing bewilderment. Martin would almost have preferred anger or denunciation. He knew that he would never forget that look as long as he lived.

When the doctor had finished examining Martin for the second time, Andrew came back into the bedroom and lingered there for a while. He made desultory conversation for a few minutes, and then turned to look out of the window and said, "It was meant for me, you know, that bullet."

"Yes," Martin said. "I guessed that."

"They sent me a note, a couple of weeks ago. The IRA. Telling me I was under sentence of death. I chose to ignore it. I wasn't going to let them have me on the run like a criminal, afraid of my own shadow. But I should have told my parents, at least . . . taken more care. I thought it would be in Dublin, you see, if they tried to kill me. I should have realised that by being here I was putting you all at risk – my mother, Catherine, the guests ... anything could have happened."

Martin said nothing, turning over the edge of the counterpane in his fingers. The IRA would find out soon enough that they had got the wrong man, he knew; Andrew would not be able to rest easy.

"So, but for your bad luck," Andrew said with a forced laugh, "I might be lying dead now."

Martin looked up. "And but for Aunt Madge's blessed cat, I'd be lying dead. I must get that cat a plateful of chicken, at the very least, or whatever cats like best."

Catherine came in to see him a little later on, but she had obviously been instructed not to tire him, and went away again after a few minutes.

Alone with his thoughts, Martin was aware of a strange and quite unfamiliar feeling of calm, almost of content. It was as if the shooting had purged him, bringing back the memories he had tried to escape, but finally leaving him clear-headed. He had, at least, faced up to his inadequacies; if it was not easy to acknowledge, at least he was no longer trying to hide it from himself.

He lay back and looked out of the window at

the hazy, cloud-streaked sky with a curious feeling of starting afresh, of having cast off an old dead skin, like a snake. The bullet had been meant for Andrew: Andrew had said so, and Martin had already worked that out for himself. And yet in some strange way he felt as if it must have been a sign for him, the bullet he had been owed for three years, the one he deserved for letting Panton go to his death, and for not dying with Overstone, for not going obediently to his death as a dutiful officer should. But Fate had intervened again, as before when it had sent him blundering into the German trench. He had survived the bullet, by another fluke. Martin did not consider himself to be superstitious, but now he felt that Fate's second intervention must be intended as some sort of omen, or signal. He was meant to live, and to go on living.

From this new, optimistic perspective he considered all the time he had wasted, the opportunities he had missed. He had a whole life ahead of him. He was young and in good health, he was reasonably wealthy, he had a comfortable home and a loving family, and there was a career waiting for him as soon as he chose to take it up. Hundreds of thousands of men had come out of the war with far, far less.

There was one important thing missing, however. She had been there all the time, if only he hadn't been such a blinkered idiot. If it weren't for the doctor's specific instructions he would have climbed out of bed straight away, to get moving, to get started on his purposeful new life. He would go to her and tell her, try to explain. She would understand, he knew she would; all along, she had been the one person he should have confided in, telling her everything instead of brooding alone. In his imagination they were already together; he could see her blue eyes looking at him in that familiar tender way, and could almost feel her soft hair and smell the perfume of her skin as she embraced him . . .

He took her photograph out of his wallet and looked at it for the first time in months.

In the late afternoon, Catherine was allowed to join him, bringing with her a tray of tea things.

"How are you feeling?" she asked him.

"Fine."

She looked at him doubtfully.

"I do," he said. "In fact, it sounds ridiculous but I feel better than I did before."

She laughed at him, putting down the tray and sitting in the upright chair by the window. "I must remember that. If ever I feel off-colour I must arrange to be shot in the head and dunked in the pond. It must do wonders for the constitution."

"Seriously, though," he said, "it seems to have sorted things out in my mind. There's nothing like thinking you could easily have been dead for making you see things in perspective."

She poured him a cup of tea and moved across to put it on his bedside table. "So what have you sorted out?"

"Sit here for a minute. I'll get a crick in my neck talking to you if you stay over there." He moved his legs aside for her, just as he had on the previous occasion, and she sat down carefully. Then he said, "Mainly, it's made me realise that I've spent far too long dwelling on the past. It's time to pick up the pieces and carry on. As soon as I get over this."

"You mean go back to England? Take up your job?"

"Yes. That, and something else as well. But if I tell you, you won't tell anyone else yet, will you? Not yet."

She smiled. "All right. It's a secret."

He hesitated and then took her hand in both of his. "I've decided that I shall go back to Serena. I want to marry her after all. I realise now that it's what I've wanted all along."

Catherine said nothing for a moment. She looked tired and wan, and he realised that she must be suffering from the shock of last night. She had seen what happened, Andrew had told him. He waggled her hand in his, and she looked up at him. "Don't you think it's a good idea?"

She smiled and said, "I think it's a lovely idea, Martin, really I do. You deserve to be happy, after all you've gone through. This, on top of everything else."

He laughed, and kissed her on the cheek. She really was very sweet. "I knew you'd be pleased. You must meet Serena one day, when you're back at school in England. I'm sure you'd get on well together."

"I'd like that."

She drank her tea, and they chatted for a bit longer, and then she got up and said that she ought to leave him to rest. For once, their roles were reversed, and she seemed to be the one with something on her mind which she would not tell him. He supposed it was the shock, and her worry about Andrew.

Riddle Me This

Andrew went back to Dublin early on Monday, and in the afternoon Delia went with the Frasers to Kingstown, to see them off on the Holyhead boat. The colonel, who had clearly found it difficult to play the role of congenial host since the shooting, went gratefully into his study on the pretext of doing the accounts.

Catherine could not bear to be in the house for another day. At least her mother's absence gave her the chance of slipping away; had Delia been present, with her new awareness of the risks they all faced, it would have been far more difficult to leave the house. Catherine knew that they would have to be a good deal less complacent than they had been, but first she had to go down to the village, and she had to go alone. She would probably be back before her father noticed that she was missing; just in case, not wanting him to think she had been kidnapped by gunmen, she told Martin that she was going out for a short while. It meant leaving Martin on his own, still under doctor's orders not to get up for another day or two, but he had had out a pen and writing paper when she went into his room and she imagined he would be perfectly happy writing to the unsuspecting Serena. He would be going back home as soon as he was fit enough, and Catherine thought it likely that her mother, thoroughly unnerved by Saturday's incident, would spend more time in England too, once Martin had gone and the school term had begun; the Frasers had already invited her to stay with them for as long as she liked. Catherine thought of her father spending lonely hours in his study, and felt sad for him. Their way of life was going, irretrievably.

It was hard to believe so as she walked down the narrow road towards the village between familiar fields and woods. The meadow beside the lane was bright with wild flowers: purple vetches, and scabious, and clover which hummed with foraging bees. Three fields away she could see a horse standing patiently harnessed to a wagon, while two farm workers loaded stooks of corn. The sun was shining behind heavy clouds, to dramatic effect; a white cottage at the top of the field stood sharply illuminated against a dark, almost purple sky. Catherine realised that she should have brought a raincoat, but it was too late to go back now. Summer was fading.

The rowan trees at the edge of the Mullaghclee-vaun woods carried thick clusters of berries, and the long grasses by the roadside were dried and yellowish. Catherine thought of misty autumn mornings, and cobwebs draped in the hedge-rows, and turf-smoke and dark evenings at home . . . but dark evenings would never be the same again.

The sun slid behind brimming clouds so heavy that the sky seemed to sag with their weight. It began to rain, great drops spitting down at the parched ground, so that the air smelled of damp-ened dust and earth. For shelter, Catherine kept close to the trees at the side of the road, hearing the steady patter on leaves as the rain increased. As she approached the village, the edge of the Mullaghcleevaun woods curved away, neatly fenced, leaving her exposed in the open. The rain fell heavily now with the surprising ferocity of a summer cloudburst, no longer in drops but in cold hard rods, making her gasp. She ran, and it felt like breasting a waterfall; the village was almost obliterated from view. Her feet squelched in her shoes as she ran down the gurgling water-course of the last incline towards the cottages huddled against the downpour.

In all her life at Mullaghcleevaun, she had never set foot in Jimmy Doyle's forge. It was a lean-to building, attached to a house, with double doors open to a cluttered yard. Catherine splashed through the puddles towards it. Perversely, now that she had reached shelter, the rain began to ease up a little.

The forge was a haven of warmth. A big fire blazed, radiating heat to Catherine's streaming face as she hesitated inside the door. A black farm horse was tied up inside, dozing peacefully, occasionally flicking an ear. Conor had his back to the outside yard. He was stooped, knees braced, over one of the horse's huge hind feet which he held in his lap, and was rasping vigorously. There was no one else in the forge, to Catherine's relief.

Conor lowered the hoof to the ground and straightened up rather stiffly, giving the horse's rump an affectionate slap, and then he turned and saw Catherine. He stared at her speechlessly and she realised what a strange apparition she must seem, half-drenched, quite apart from the fact that this was the last place he would expect to see her.

"Jesus, Mary and Joseph!" The rasp clanged to the floor and he came over to her, reaching out a hand to feel the wetness of her sleeve, and her hair. "What are you doing? You shouldn't have come here. Is there an accident?"

"No, I came to see you. To talk."

He stared at her, his initial expression of

surprise replaced by something more guarded. She saw that he knew well enough why she had come. His glance travelled down her body, taking in the soaked dress which clung to her legs, and her mud-splashed stockings and shoes. He tugged gently at her arm. "Come over to the fire. You'll be catching your death."

There was an upturned barrel for her to sit on, and he fetched a jute horse-rug which smelled of animal warmth, and draped it around her shoulders. Then he stood in front of her, undecided. He wore a white shirt open at the neck and a leather apron which reached almost to his ankles; his face was flushed with exertion and heat.

"Would you wait while I finish this shoeing? I won't be long. They're coming to take the horse back at three. You can be drying out a bit."

"All right." Now that she had arrived, she felt reluctant to begin the conversation, afraid of what she might find out. She shivered by the fire, her chilled limbs slowly relaxing as the horse-rug became a cave of warmth, steaming gently. The air smelled of horse and of singed hoof. She watched Conor as he worked, moving from the fire to the anvil to beat a shoe into shape, then lowering it into a bucket of water to cool. The horse moved obligingly to his commands, adjusting its balance to lift a hindleg for him. He held the shoe to its hoof, but was dissatisfied with its fit, and brought it back to heat again, holding it into the fire with the tongs. She looked at his sunburned, capable hands, remembering their light hold on the reins in front of her, and their gentle touch, smoothing her hair. Had the same hands steadied a rifle, swinging it round to follow Martin's progress across the lawn . . . had his calloused fingers squeezed the trigger, firing the shot intended to kill? It was impossible to believe it; she did not want to believe it, if she were honest. It was easier to switch off her mind, to sit here in her damp steaming clothes, and to listen to the clang of iron and the scrape of shod hooves on the stone floor. It was reassuring to see Conor at work, handling the tools and the horse with equal firmness and assurance.

It was preferable to thinking about what he might do when he was not at work. She felt that she had been incredibly stupid, not to have guessed; he had been open enough about the bitterness of his feelings. She had not mentioned her suspicions to anyone, not even Patsy. Patsy considered herself a nationalist, Catherine knew, but did not approve of violence as a means to an end.

Conor stretched the horse's leg forward to give the clenches of the nails a final buffing. The shoeing was finished, and she could delay no longer. He fastened a nosebag to the horse's face and sat down near her on an upturned box, saying nothing.

"I came to ask you about the shooting on Saturday," she said.

"I know." He was looking at the horse, not at her, his profile stern.

"You know it was Martin who . . . who got hit, not Andrew?"

"Yes, I do. I'm sorry."

"You're sorry! How can you say that when you . . . when you . . ." She could not bring herself to say the words. Her voice dropped to a whisper. "Conor, was it you who . . . did you . . . were you the gunman?"

"I was not." His eyes met hers for a moment, and she tried to read his expression, a mixture of reproach and wariness. He bent forward, elbows on his knees, picking at a broken thumbnail, turning slightly away from her so that she could see only the lashes of one downcast eye and the glint of stubble on his cheek. Relief swept over her, but she knew that it was not simply a matter of acceptance or denial.

"But you . . . A stranger wouldn't have known where to go, or when . . . and the shot came from the cottage. You . . . you must have had something to do with it."

He looked round at her and nodded, almost

imperceptibly. She had known, illogically, that he would not lie to her.

"But not my father," he said quickly. "He knew nothing about it. Till afterwards. He guessed soon enough."

"Andrew said it must have been someone who knows the house well, and its routines," Catherine said. "But neither he nor Father have suspected you ... they trust you. You knew Andrew goes into the garden to smoke. I suppose you found out from one of the servants that he'd be at home on Saturday, or from your father ..."

"I did not. You told me so yourself."

She stared at him, realising. "I remember," she said slowly. "I did tell you. But I'd never have guessed you'd ... Oh, Conor, how could you betray Andrew like that, betray all of us?"

He looked at her coldly. "It wasn't as you think. It wasn't my decision. He was under sentence of death from the time he took up his post at the Castle. That had nothing to do with me. My job was to pass on information."

"But how could you do it? After my father's been good to you ... you said so, those were your own words, you had nothing against him ... Couldn't you have refused, done some other ... some other job instead?"

His expression changed. "I'm sorry it had to

be your family, Catherine, truly I am. But I couldn't refuse. I've taken the oath. Those were my orders."

"Oath? What oath?"

"To the Irish Republican Army," he said. He raised his head as he said it, with an unmistakeable flash of pride. "I couldn't go back on it. You can't commit yourself to a cause and then wriggle out of it the moment you have to do something unpleasant."

"But ..." She struggled to find words. "Oaths, orders? Does that mean you can't make up your own mind? Do you have to do everything you're told?"

The horse grated a hoof on the floor and snorted, blowing a spray of oats out of the nosebag.

"You have to trust the people in command," Conor said. "They depend on ordinary people, to be their eyes and ears. Not obeying orders would mean being disloyal, being a traitor."

"You talk about loyalty ... But if carrying out orders means betraying someone who's been kind to you ...?"

"Kind, yes. Your father can afford to be kind to me. He's done well out of this country, the way things are. But if you're going to talk about betrayal you ought to look a bit nearer home."

"What do you mean?"

For the first time it occurred to her that perhaps she ought to feel afraid of him. He was, after all, on one side, and she – even if through circumstance rather than choice – on the other; it appeared that sides had to be taken, however reluctantly. But in spite of the bitterness of his words, she could not feel afraid. He was still Conor.

"Have you no idea what your brother's job is?" he said.

"Intelligence, he told me. Administration. Paperwork."

"That's a useful name to put to it. I suppose you've heard of the reprisals – how each time there's a shooting, the Black and Tans go out with guns and cans of petrol, and kill innocent people? Last week, in Kilcarbery, they killed a family man who'd done no harm to anyone. They bayoneted him to death, in his own home."

She stared at him, appalled.

"Isn't that betrayal?" he said fiercely, "betraying the ordinary Irish people they're here to protect? Your brother's own countrymen?"

"But what has that to do with Andrew?"

"He has informers planted," Conor said. "They supply him with the names, and he passes them on. And sometimes any name will do."

Catherine did not want to think of what was involved in Andrew's job, not now. Instead, she said, "That RIC man, the one who was shot in the woods above our house ... were you involved in that, as well?"

"No. I've never shot anyone, not yet. But I will if I have to."

His words chilled her, for all she had suspected it.

"I thought, the other night," he went on, "that you were beginning to see how it is. For us, in our own country, to be ruled by a foreign power, to have the English lording it over us, when they have no more right here than the Kaiser of Germany. And now they've brought over the Tans and the Auxiliaries, men who are in it for money, and couldn't give a damn for Ireland or the Irish people. The kind of thing they're doing – burning, killing – it's what the Germans were doing in Belgium at the start of the war. It's what the war was about – it's what Fergal died for. And now the same thing's happening here, and the British government won't even admit to it, let alone lift a finger to stop it – " He was staring intently at the fire, so that his eyes blazed with reflected twin flames. "Can you be surprised if we fight them back the only way we can?"

"No, I'm not ... I mean ... in principle, I agree with you," she faltered, "but ... but principles are one thing, human lives are another ..." Her thoughts were too muddled to be put adequately into words.

He looked at her. "You're wrong there. You can't separate principles from living, or dying. I knew that when I took the oath. Something as big as that, as important, it *is* your life, your whole life. Nothing else matters."

She heard the conviction in his voice, and sensed the taut energy of his body. It made her feel inadequate. What was there in her own life to inspire such passion, such complete, uncompromising surrender to a cause? She remembered what Maura had said, about their lives being filled with trivialities to avoid ever having to confront the lack of real purpose. Conor had a purpose. She could see the attraction, she thought, of wanting something so desperately that you were prepared to die for it. But at the same time she saw how dangerous it could be to devote yourself so utterly to a cause, submitting to the judgment of a higher authority. It could easily be a handing over of responsibility; because you saw your own life as expendable, it would be easy to think that other people's were, too. In that strangely exalted frame of mind any orders could seem justifiable, no matter how abhorrent.

"Does it matter to you," she asked, "that you could have had the wrong man killed? Or is that just one of the risks?"

"I'm sorry about your man there, Catherine, your cousin. I was glad when my Da told me he was only wounded – "

"Isn't that just as bad as the Black and Tans killing the wrong man?" she flared. "But I suppose Martin's English, though, so he'll do just as well?"

He did not answer directly, but said instead, "I hope it won't be a lasting injury."

"Thank you," she said, with biting sarcasm.

She looked towards the yard outside. The rain had cleared to a fine drizzle, the sun filtering through. A few brown chickens were pecking around in the yard. At the sides of the blacksmith's shed, pieces of wrought-ironwork in various stages of completion were stacked against the wall: gates, fire-sets, door knockers. Jimmy Doyle made all sorts of things besides horse shoes, and she remembered that this same forge had reputedly supplied pikes for Wolfe Tone's rebellions, nearly a hundred years ago. Some things did not change, she thought: the English were still keeping the Irish in brutal suppression, the Irish fighting back, with the spirit of defiance bred into them over the centuries.

"I shan't stay here much longer," Conor said. "I like it well enough here at the forge, but it makes things difficult for my father. I don't want him to lose his job. I'm thinking of moving down to join one of the Cork Brigades. But then," he added, "maybe I won't be free to make the choice, not now."

She thought for the first time of his situation, realising what he was implying. "You mean if I tell Andrew what you've told me, or go to the RIC? No, I won't do that."

"I don't know why you'd be wanting to do me any favours." He stoked the fire, stirring the bright coals so that sparks showered up.

"It's not that. But I don't want you to come to any harm either."

Looked at objectively, it was a ridiculous thing to say to someone who wanted her brother dead, but she meant it. She had a clear enough idea now of what the result could be if she mentioned Conor's name in connection with the shooting. He had not fired a shot, but that could easily turn out to be a minor detail, if he were picked up by the Tans or the Auxiliaries.

"I don't suppose I shall see you again," he said. He was standing close to her, looking at her in a way she remembered. She thought of him jumping down from Shamie in the dusk beneath the trees, kissing her. In spite of everything, the sweetness of the memory disturbed her.

"I trusted you, as well as Father," she said bitterly. "I suppose . . . that evening when we did the whitewashing, and went in the woods

. . . you thought it would be a chance to get information from me. No more than that."

He looked at her reproachfully. His green eyes were sad, just as they had been then, flickering with amber lights. "No, Caitlin. It wasn't like that at all. I – "

He reached out a hand to touch the side of her face. She stood up quickly, and his arm dropped. She did not trust herself, in this confused intensity of feeling. She thought she would cry if she stayed any longer, and she would not cry in front of Conor. Not now.

"Be careful in Cork, then – " God, what a stupid, meaningless thing to say.

"It's goodbye, so," he said.

"Yes." She hesitated for a moment, and then said lightly, "What will you do when you've got your independent Ireland? What will there be to die for then?"

If Conor said anything in reply, she did not wait to hear it. She gave him back the horse-rug, and left.

We Ourselves

When Martin was allowed out of bed for the first time, he told Catherine that he wanted to go upstairs to see Aunt Madge.

"You never know how much the old girl takes in," he explained. "I thought she'd like to know that one of her infernal cats saved my skin."

Pleased with his idea, Catherine said, "I'll come with you. But she probably won't know who you are. She'll think you're Edwin, and I'm Clarissa from Bombay, or something. And that bandage round your head will confuse her even more."

"Who is Edwin?"

"I don't know. She's always going on about him. Perhaps we can find out, get her to tell us."

However, Phyllis showed them into Aunt Madge's sitting room and said, "She's having her afternoon sleep, I'm afraid. She gets very tired."

"We'll come back another time, then," Martin said, turning to go.

"Wait." Catherine's attention was caught by

the photographs on the walls. Wedding groups, formal portraits, army officers in uniform, shooting parties with rows of dead birds laid out on the ground; all preserved in sepia tint or black and white, framed and mounted. Like butterflies pinned to a board, Catherine thought, faded and dead, but still evoking past glories; a different generation, a way of life that had seemed stable and enduring to those who lived it – as permanent as the Anglo-Irish ascendancy had seemed to her father's generation.

"Are there any photographs of Edwin here?" she asked.

Phyllis looked surprised. "Most of them are in her room, my dear. But I think he's in one of these wedding groups. Let me see – " She put on her reading spectacles and moved along the wall, scrutinising the rows of Victorian faces. "Yes, here he is." She pointed to a man in a high-collared suit, with meticulously parted hair and a thick moustache. "That's Edwin."

Catherine moved closer. In spite of the Victorian clothes and stilted pose, the man smiled out of the photograph at her like an older, somewhat dandified version of Martin. She could understand Aunt Madge's confusion. She said so to Martin, but he frowned at the photograph and said that he could see no likeness at all.

"Here, this is a better one." Phyllis had pushed

a slim black cat out of the way to rummage in the scroll-top desk. "It's a copy of the one she's got framed on her bedside table. He was her fiancée, you see."

Phyllis handed over a large photograph in an oval mounting. The picture was a formal portrait, obviously posed in a studio, to judge by the careful drapings behind the couple, and an elegant potted palm. The moustached man and a lady who must be Aunt Madge stood close together, their heads turned to look at each other. She had one hand resting on his sleeve, nonchalantly stretched to show the cluster of diamonds on the ring finger. Catherine could see from the hawk-like nose and imperious eyebrows that this was indeed Aunt Madge at perhaps thirty or thirty-five, not a youthful bride-to-be by any means; the lines of the querulous old lady's face, familiar to Catherine, were already beginning to appear. Aunt Madge's features were too austere to be beautiful, but her expression as she gazed at Edwin transfigured her, so that this was clearly not an attitude adopted for the conventional engagement photograph, but something real and enduring.

"But what happened to them?" Martin said. "She never married, did she?"

"Edwin died," Phyllis said. "He'd inherited a property out in Kenya, and he and your aunt were going to live there and run it as a farm, growing coffee. Edwin went on ahead to make arrangements before they were married, and he contracted cholera and died of it."

"Poor Aunt Madge," Catherine said, thinking she knew how her aunt must have felt. She had never thought of it before: the passions and sorrows which seemed solely her own had afflicted generations and generations past, as joyous and as wrenching as they were now. She looked again at the photograph, thinking that the hand which lay casually on Edwin's arm was the same gnarled one which now teased knots out of cats' fur, and the face so soft and radiant with love was now weathered and deeply lined.

Martin took the photograph from her and studied it carefully. Catherine looked at his dark brows and the curve of his cheekbone, and the feeling of love and loss gripped her like a physical pain, all mixed up with her feelings for Conor, equally misplaced, equally hopeless. She wondered whether he was thinking of Serena, and she imagined Serena looking at him just as Aunt Madge was looking at Edwin in the picture, in a way which excluded everyone else.

"She always kept his letters and photographs. But it's only recently she's started to talk about him, getting confused in her mind. She never forgot him, you see," Phyllis said simply.

Catherine was surprised and moved by the powerful emotion contained in this quiet corner of the house. Was it tragedy, or triumph, she wondered? Tragedy, that thirty or forty years had been spent in mourning for a ghost; or triumph, that Aunt Madge's love for Edwin had endured, refusing to be tempered by the brutal suddenness of death? She did not know, but felt her own sorrow first sharpened by it, and then humbled. She had lost her loves, both of them; each in his own way had let her down. But reason told her that she had let herself down, by expecting too much, seeing them as she had wished to see them, rather than as they really were. Perhaps Aunt Madge had done the same with Edwin, but no one would ever know. The smiling couple in the photograph remained inviolable.

When she heard that Maura was coming to spend an afternoon at Mullaghcleevaun, Catherine found that she was looking forward to the occasion. Maura, she thought, was the one person who would understand how she felt; Maura would help her to sort out the confusion of loyalties and half-formed convictions which her brain felt too feeble to disentangle. Their quarrel seemed irrelevant now, no more than a schoolgirls' squabble.

They went out to the terrace. It was a fine but windy afternoon, the trees tossing their heads beneath a sky piled with towering cumulus. The garden smelled fresh and clean after the heavy rain. Some of the taller perennials in the border lay flattened to the ground, their pale blue petals scattered in the grass like tiny pieces of sky; the colonel, dispirited, had neither found the time to stake them up nor sent Paddy Kerrigan out to do so.

Martin sat with them for a while, but then said he was going indoors to write letters, and left them alone.

"He's going back to England, to get married," Catherine explained. "To Serena, the girl he was engaged to before."

Maura looked at her quizzically. "I see. Has Serena agreed? After he let her down before?"

"Well, no. He hasn't told her yet."

"Ask might be a more appropriate word. Her opinion on the subject is rather important, after all. I'm sure he thinks he only has to say, as if she's spent all this time waiting for him to change his mind."

Catherine was about to take up Martin's defence, from force of habit, but she stopped herself. He did seem to have taken Serena's acceptance for granted, as if no girl in her right mind would hesitate.

"Do you mind?" Maura asked. "If he does marry her?"

"No. Yes. I don't know . . . I thought I would have minded terribly, and in a way I do. But it seems inevitable, part of everything changing and moving on, this summer." Catherine suddenly did not want to dwell on her foolishness over Martin. Her foolishness over Conor she would keep to herself. "Mother's going to stay in England with the Frasers as soon as Martin's gone, and I'm back at school," she said instead. "I think . . . I think she and Father may end up living apart. She wants Andrew to give up his job here and get a safer army posting, in England, or in India. I hope he will, too. I don't feel very proud of what he does here, now that I – now that I know a bit more about it. But I don't want him to come to any harm."

"No." Maura understood.

"Mother doesn't really belong here, and Father will never leave. This troublesome little country, Mother calls it. She still sees herself as English. What's happening here is just a nuisance to her, an inconvenience."

"I know. It's easier to run away. My parents have argued about it, too. And I suppose we'll be doing the same, won't we? Running back to England."

"But not through choice." Catherine thought

without enthusiasm of the dusty classrooms and comfortless dormitories of Kingswood House, and the uninspired lessons which awaited her, just a few weeks away. She would cope with it, because she was intellectually undemanding, but she could understand how stifling it must be for Maura.

"One thing I have convinced my parents of," Maura said, following the same train of thought, "is that I'm going to take a scholarship to a women's college. Miss Samuels is going to help me. I've no intention of becoming a decorative young lady, doing the London season. I'm not equipped for it, anyway."

Catherine looked at her. No, Maura was not decorative, but she had a quiet strength which Catherine envied.

"What will you do?" she asked. "After you've been to college, I mean?"

"I want to be a member of Parliament," Maura said.

Catherine almost laughed out loud, realising just in time that Maura meant it. "A member of Parliament?" she repeated. "At Westminster?"

"No, of course not. A member of the Irish parliament. The Dail. When it really is the Irish Parliament. I want to do something, in some way, to help make a new Ireland. I expect you

270

think it sounds ridiculous," Maura said, accurately enough.

"Can women be members of Parliament?"

"Of course they can. Constance Markiewicz is already Minister for Labour in the Dail. Don't you read the newspapers?" Maura said, with a touch of her old asperity.

"But the Dail is illegal." Catherine did know that much.

"It won't always be illegal. Not when the British give in."

Maura sounded quite certain about it. Catherine was silent, aware once again how purposeless her own life was. Everyone else had some clear goal: Martin to take up his job and marry Serena, Conor to join the Cork Brigade and fight for Ireland, Maura to pursue her education ... Maura wanted to fight for Ireland too, Catherine recognised, in a way entirely different from Conor's; shaping the future, not dwelling on the violence of the present and the injustices of the past ... Perhaps Maura's idea was no more than a schoolgirl's soaring ambition, unrealistic and unattainable, but nevertheless Catherine felt it worth reaching for.

"What will you do?" Maura said. "If your parents decide to live apart, I mean? You might have to make a difficult choice."

"No, there's no choice," Catherine said, suddenly sure of it. "If it comes to choosing between Mother and England, or Father and Ireland, my mind's made up already. I want to live in Ireland, no matter how uncertain the future is here. And I want to be Irish, not Anglo-Irish. All that old injustice – it's gone on for too long. There must be something better, something more . . . more equal."

Further than that, she had not thought. But Maura smiled, approving.

"So it's Sinn Fein from now on," she said.

"What? You're going to join Sinn Fein?"

"No. Not the party. Not yet, at any rate. But what it means . . . *we ourselves* . . . it seems like a good motto, for us. We can't go on as our parents have done, letting them make our decisions, doing what's expected of us. We have to make the pattern for our own lives."

"Yes," Catherine said.

She had not expected to feel optimistic. Everything was breaking up, everyone going away. Her sense of loss was acute, stinging her painfully in unguarded moments. And for all Maura's talk of a new Ireland, the situation was no less desperate; the feelings on both sides were as bitter as they had ever been. Whether Maura's idea of a peaceful, self-governing country would ever come into being, and what her own place in it might be, she could only guess. But this was her country, and her future was bound up with it. The house behind her was warm and solid, absorbing the sunshine. She looked down at the grass sloping down to the pond, and the woods below, with a strong sense of belonging. The sun was warm on her face and the wind pulled gently at her hair, and she felt strangely at peace, in spite of everything. Swifts were flying low over the garden, as fast and direct as arrows, their streamlined wings curved into taut dark shapes against the rippled background of the pond. One of Aunt Madge's cats stalked across the lawn towards the house, high-stepping, placing its paws in the grass with precision, and Catherine smiled.

Hard and Fast by Linda Newbery
£3.99

When Melanie organises a sponsored fast at school, she has no idea of the effect it will have on her friends. Each of the main characters discovers something about themselves, so that by the end of the story rather more than funds for the starving has been achieved.

With strong characterisation and excellent dialogue, Linda Newbery's novel has both sensitivity and style.

Run with the Hare by Linda Newbery
£3.50

A sensitive and authentic novel exploring the workings of an animal rights group, through the eyes of Elaine, a sixth-form pupil. Elaine becomes involved with the group through her more forceful friend Kate, and soon becomes involved with Mark, an Adult Education student and one of the more sophisticated members of the group. Elaine finds herself painting slogans and sabotaging a fox hunt. Then she and her friends uncover a dog fighting ring – and things turn very nasty.

Children of Winter
by Berlie Doherty £2.99

Catherine and her family are walking in the
Derbyshire countryside when a sudden storm breaks
out. They are forced to take shelter in an old barn.
Somehow she remembers sheltering there before, from
something far more dangerous than a storm.

Granny Was a Buffer Girl
by Berlie Doherty
(Winner of the 1987 Carnegie Medal)
£2.75

Before she sets off for a year's adventure in France, Jess
wants to share all the family secrets – three generations
of emotion, love and experience.

Spellhorn
by Berlie Doherty £2.99

Blind Laura has followed Spellhorn the unicorn to join
the Wild Ones on their journey to their beloved
Wilderness. But Laura has to return to her home, and
to do so she must fight against Flight, her bitterest
enemy, and cross the dreaded Sea of Snakes.

Come a Stranger
by Cynthia Voigt £3.50

For Mina, the scholarship to Ballet School summer camp was the most marvellous experience in her life. But in her second year she is ungainly and clumsy and after only a few weeks she is asked to leave. Mina thinks she has been rejected because she is black and her once sunny world is clouded with uncertainty.

Sons from Afar
by Cynthia Voigt £3.50

James and Sammy Tillerman's father walked out when they were very young, so long ago that Sammy can't understand why James is interested in him. But James desperately needs to find out what kind of man his father was.

Seventeen Against the Dealer
by Cynthia Voigt £3.50

The final book in the Tillerman saga. Dicey is now trying to earn her own living as a boatbuilder despite demands made on her by her family. A drifter turns up at the workshop offering his help, and Dicey comes to trust him, letting him work with her and enjoying his company. But problems at home and at work overwhelm her, and she ends up trusting him too much.

Jackaroo
by Cynthia Voigt £3.50

In a distant time and a far-off place there were legends of Jackaroo, the masked hero who rode at night, giving aid to the helpless and money to the destitute. Gwyn the Innkeeper's daughter finds his costume and uses it for her own ends.

The Callender Papers
by Cynthia Voigt £2.99

In the summer of 1894, twelve-year-old Jean Wainwright goes to work for Mr Thiel, cataloguing assorted business and personal papers of his late wife's family. As she works through the papers, she finds clues to a terrible family story. Worse still, Jean realises that the more she learns, the more dangerous her own position becomes.

Tell Me if the Lovers are Losers
by Cynthia Voigt £2.99

Nothing in her boarding school could have prepared Ann Garder for her roommates at college, Niki and Hildy. Their only common interest is volleyball, but this provides a centre for their friendship, and helps to give Ann the strength she needs when tragedy strikes.

Some Other War
Linda Newbery

Seventeen-year-old twins Jack and Alice have their lives mapped out. Jack is a stable lad at the Morlands' country house, and Alice is chambermaid to Madeleine Morland. Had it not been for the First World War, they might have stayed there all their lives. But the war changed many things, and brought Jack and Alice independence from the rigid social structure of the times.

Jack joins up with the first flush of enthusiasm, and is sent to the trenches. Alice continues at the Morlands', but as the casualties mount up and it becomes obvious the war will not be over by Christmas, she feels she must do something to help and begins working as a nurse.

Linda Newbery's novel accurately and sympathetically portrays life at the time of the Great War through the eyes of young people.

£3.99

A Summer to Die
by Lois Lowry
£2.99

Having a sister who is blonde and pretty and popular can be tricky if you're like Meg – serious, hardworking and, well, plain. But when Molly becomes critically ill, Meg has to face up to something much worse than jealousy.

Number the Stars
by Lois Lowry
(Newbery Award Winner 1990)
£2.99

Copenhagen, 1943. Annemarie carries on her normal life under the shadow of the Nazis – until they begin their campaign to "relocate" the Jews of Denmark. Annemarie's best friend Ellen is a Jew, and Annemarie is called upon to help Ellen and many others escape across the sea.

Switcharound
by Lois Lowry
£3.50

Caroline and JP are not thrilled at the thought of spending the summer with their father. On a scale of 1 to 10, with nuclear war as 10, JP gives it 8, Caroline 9. But things are never quite as bad as they seem...or are they?

ORDER FORM

To order direct from the publishers, just make a list of the titles you want and fill in the form below:

Name_____

Address_____

_____

_____

Send to: Dept 6, HarperCollins Publishers Ltd, Westerhill Road, Bishopbriggs, Glasgow G64 2QT.

Please enclose a cheque or postal order to the value of the cover price, plus:

UK & BFPO: Add £1.00 for the first book, and 25p per copy for each addition book ordered.

Overseas and Eire: Add £2.95 service charge. Books will be sent by surface mail but quotes for airmail despatch will be given on request.

A 24-hour telephone ordering service is available to Visa and Access card holders:
041-772 2281